I0667963

TURTLE CROAKIES

SAM CHEEVER

ELECTRIC PROSE PUBLICATIONS

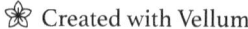 Created with Vellum

A frog, a cat, and a hobgoblin walk into a bar...in the Jurassic period. Nope...not kidding. Okay, maybe it wasn't really a bar. But it was definitely the local drinking establishment. For dinosaurs...

My old mentor, Alice Parker is back, and she's brought a problem with her. A big one. One that's already testing the sprite's ability to keep it in lettuce and strawberries.

It turns out that Alice has been on the run for a minute, trying to protect a magical tortoise from a dangerous sorceress who wants it for herself. You might be wondering why anybody would want to steal a tortoise. Well, if you had the chance to travel through time at the push of a button, or rather the press of a turtle's shell, would you take it?

Yeah, me neither. I have enough trouble dealing with *this* time and world... But clearly, we aren't all diabolical magic users bent on our own empowerment. I mean, the possibilities for evil are unending if one can time-hop at will.

Luckily, I have two cats, two frogs, and a hobgoblin to help me stave off the latest crisis. The only question is...what am I going to do with a former KoA who was as ineffectual at the Keeper's job as the goddess's torn pantyhose are at holding water. The only thing she'd been worse at was training me!

And, more importantly, now that she's here...how am I going to get rid of her?

Holy turtle trousers, this Keeper gig gets more challenging by the day...or the millennia!

1

BOB'S YOUR FROG-FLIPPIN' UNCLE

We should have never left Croakies unattended. I realized that now. But when I received an order to retrieve a cursed girdle that makes its wearer gain instant weight and then resists being removed, my personal sensibilities wouldn't allow me to put off its retrieval.

I'd had trouble enough with my own weight to ignore such an unkind artifact. I was pretty sure my wide backside had nothing to do with the donuts, tacos, and brownies I'd been eating on a regular basis. No. That couldn't be it. I'd just been born with a slow metabolism.

Yes, I had.

The long and the short of it was, I could just as easily have been the one donning that cruel latex and magic prison, instead of the woman who'd been trapped by it.

And, to be fair, I'd had no way of knowing it would take me and my friends three hours to pry that poor woman out of the grabby girdle. If Rustin hadn't thought of the flame thrower option, we might still be fighting with the thing.

It wasn't as bad as it sounds. The woman, who'd been a bridge troll, would recover from lightly toasted buns. But she wouldn't have recovered from instantly gaining fifty pounds.

I mean, who would? One needs to build up to that kind of thing, preferably via lots of tasty goodies.

Anywho... back to my problem.

Imagine my surprise when we finally returned to find Croakies had been infiltrated.

I stared at the monster in the center of the bookstore, some of the tension leaching out of my muscles as it stared back at me, its jaws lazily munching the lunch salad Sebille had thrown at it.

My lunch salad, blast her evil sprite ways. Like it wasn't hard enough trying to lose weight. Now she was throwing my tasteless, diet lunch at every Tom, Dick, and Turtle who wandered in off the street.

The sprite was crouched near the small refrigerator from which she'd pilfered the ill-gotten garden castoff. She held Mr. Slimy in her hands, clutching him close in case the monster decided the little green squish looked good enough to eat.

Standing near the door that divided the bookstore from the magical artifact library in back, my friend Rustin had his hands on his hips and was observing the creature with mute fascination.

Our resident hobgoblin, Hobs, was perched on top of the nearest bookshelf, his eyes the size of soccer balls.

My adorable gray cat, Mr. Wicked, sat two feet away from the monster's grinding jaws, tidily folded into a watching position. His orange gaze was perfectly serene.

"How in the world did *that* get into the store?" my best friend Lea asked. "And what in the wide, wide, world of witchery is it?"

Lea was standing on top of the table, towering above us in a frothy skirt that vibrated as her knees bashed together. Her hands were out and green-hued earth-witch energy danced on the tips of her perfectly painted fingernails.

Sebille's gaze slid Lea's way and she rolled her eyes. "Haven't you ever seen a turtle, witch?"

I got the impression Lea would have glared at my cranky assistant, but that would have required that she shift her gaze from the monstrous turtle for a beat. And the world would be overrun by three-legged caterpillars before that happened.

"Technically, it's a tortoise," Mr. Slimy said in his snotty, know-it-all voice.

We ignored him because if we didn't, another giant argument about his Encyclopedia Magica ways would commence, and then we'd be off on a roller-coaster ride of verbal frog flogging for the next hour or so, completely forgetting about our unexpected and unwelcome visitor.

Suffice it to say, Slimy was enjoying acquiring the knowledge he'd missed out on in his early years when he'd been a simple frog. Unfortunately, he enjoyed thrashing us about the head and shoulders with what he'd learned nearly as much.

In the past months, he'd gained the ability to think, speak, and read like a real person from having housed Rustin's soul inside his squishy green frame. According to Rustin's powerful aunt, who was also a witch, the obnoxious green squish had absorbed some of Rustin's magical energy.

And the result? The frog was *special*. It was true. Just ask him.

"Of course I've seen turtles…" Sebille slid a quick glare toward the frog, "tortoises, before. But I've never seen one that was as big as Naida's car."

To be fair, my car wasn't really that big. It was a VW bug. Small but loveable. Still, she wasn't wrong. The tortoise was *nearly* as big as my car.

"I'm just wondering how it got through the door," Rustin said, his piercing blue gaze sliding toward the aforementioned door. "Even if you tipped him on his side, he wouldn't fit."

"What's with the different colored patches on his

back?" Sebille asked, frowning. "It looks like some-body painted him."

"Maybe it's a statue somebody animated," Lea offered.

I tilted my head, moving a few inches closer to examine the thick, wrinkly legs. "He doesn't look like he's made of metal."

"Statues don't eat salad," Sebille said.

"Apparently, neither do I," I shot back, glowering in her direction.

She rolled her eyes, putting a little extra disdain into the action to show me how much she didn't care about my lost lunch.

A toilet flushed and we jumped, all heads swiveling toward the bathroom door near Rustin. It opened a moment later, a woman walking out as she rubbed her hands dry on her long wool skirt.

"Oy, that's better," the woman said, shoving a pair of tortoiseshell spectacles back up her pugnacious nose and blinking at us from behind the thick lenses. "Sorry, we passed through Mexico on the way here, and I drank some of the water." She shook her head, the fluffy brown mess looking even less tidy than usual. Oliver, her tree frog, peeked out at us from within the brown mess. "I say, Naida, dear. You don't happen to have a spot of tea you could offer a weary traveler, do you?"

An enormous black cat trotted out of the bath-room behind her. Fenwald looked even rattier than the last time I'd seen him. The tatty black cat spotted me and gave a happy yowl, trotting heavily across the carpet to fling himself at my legs. I nearly went down under his prodigious bulk. Bending down to rub a hand over Fenny's torn ears and unkempt fur, I said, "Hello, buddy. How are you?"

"I'm afraid he had a bit of a chunder on your rug in there," the woman told me impatiently. "Do be an angel and clean it up, won't you?"

I had no idea what a *chunder* was, but it didn't sound good. Pain shot through my jaw and I realized I was clenching my teeth.

Alice Parker.

I couldn't believe she'd just shown up at Croakies without any warning. And allowed her cat to chunder in my bathroom to boot.

My erstwhile "trainer" and former Keeper of the Artifacts — a woman I hadn't heard from or spoken to in years, had walked out on me without finishing the instruction I so drastically needed. She'd all but abandoned me to my fate as a Keeper, virtually untrained and out of my league. "Alice? What are you doing here? And did you bring this with you?" I asked, pointing at the tortoise.

She leveled a beady gaze on me from behind her thick glasses. "This *is* an artifact library, is it not?"

I frowned. "Well, yes, but..."

"And you *are* a Keeper of the Artifacts, are you not?"

"Sort of..." said Sebille in a murmur that wasn't soft enough to be considered sotto voce.

I crossed my arms over my chest, taking umbrage at Alice's bossy tone of voice. "You know I am, but..."

"Well then, Bob's your Uncle." She placed her hands on her hips and grinned at me as if anything she'd just said made sense.

"Who's Bob," Slimy asked.

Rustin looked around. "Where is this Bob, Naida. And why didn't you tell us you had an uncle."

I growled. Just a little. Curling my lip back in a snarl. "There is no Bob. It's just something she says."

Lea shook her head. "If you don't mind my saying so, the British talk funny."

"Young lady," Alice said in her best imitation of an English Queen, "you are the ones who speak like barbarians. I'm speaking perfect Queen's English."

"If perfect English means flinging random Bob's around," Slimy muttered.

I coughed to hide a laugh.

Sebille rolled her eyes. "Are you saying this turtle..."

"Tortoise," said the tiny green know-it-all.

Sebille eyed the frog with a look that promised to introduce him to a French chef if he didn't button his fly-trap.

"...that the *turtle* is an artifact?" she finished.

Alice nodded. "She is. A very rare and dangerous one."

We all scanned a look over the painted bump on the rug.

The painted bump stared straight ahead with a blank look, its totally non-expressive face placid as it ground another lettuce leaf to a pulp.

We all returned our gazes to Alice, identical expressions of disbelief on our faces.

"Dangerous?" I questioned with an arch of my eyebrow. "What does it do? Bore people to death?"

Alice harrumphed. "For your information, Tildy is an Abracadabos Giant Tortoise from the Cayman Islands. A rare, magical tortoise. She's a distant relative of the Aldabra giant tortoises from the Seychelles near the east coast of Africa."

"She?" I said, surprised. "How can you tell it's a female?"

"Well, obviously her plastron is flat and her tail is shorter," Alice said in a superior tone not unlike the squishy green know-it-all's.

"Obviously," Rustin said.

I gave him a look and he grinned.

"Tildy is in grave danger. She's being stalked by a power-mad sorceress who'll stop at nothing to obtain her magic." Alice frowned. "That she-devil wants to grind the poor gentle soul into dust for a space-and-time-shifting spell and she'll stop at nothing to get her hands on Tildy."

Banshee bunions! That didn't sound good. "Have you gone to the Société?" I asked Alice.

"Of course, I have. Do you think I'm a complete idiot?"

I'd take the fifth on that one. On the grounds that Alice would smack me upside the head if I told her the truth.

"They won't help. Tildy is a non-registered living artifact. They said she needs to be registered and put under the protection of the KOA. So I brought her here."

And there you have it. Bob's your frog-flippin' uncle.

2

NOPE…NOT BITTER. NOT ME

An hour later, Lea and Rustin had returned to their respective homes. Lea lived above her Herbal Remedy shop next door, and Rustin across the street, in Sebille's old apartment. Lea had declared she needed to put together a large order of herbal tincture for an Ogre with warts. Rustin insisted he needed to get home to Sadie, his rainbow-hued amalgamate dragon, who'd once served as a soul recharger when Rustin had been without a body and looking for a solution.

Long story. His evil uncle Jacob Quilleran had ripped Rustin's soul from his body and squashed it into Mr. Slimy. It had been a magical experiment that we'd all done our best to reverse. Unfortunately, we hadn't been able to return Rustin to his body. Which was why I called him the ghost witch. He was mainly a spirit form. Although, his aunt Madeline and cousin Maude had been working on options for Rustin and had managed to infuse his spirit form with enough physicality to present as mostly solid most of the time.

It had to do with giving him a dual nature. I didn't really understand it. And we'd yet to witness Rustin's "other" side. But he was more content and mostly corporeal, so I was happy to be happy along with him.

Anyway, clearly expecting trouble, my friends had gotten out of Dodge at the first possible opportunity. Alice had given them a beady-eyed glare from behind her thick glasses when I'd tried to quiz her about the car-sized eating machine she'd parked in the middle of my bookstore.

Apparently, it was a secret.

Hobs had disappeared into the back with his buddy Slimy. And Sebille was busying herself making tea because tea was the magic elixir that transformed Alice's heart from a chunk of jagged rock to something more resembling really hard glass. Still a challenge to work with, but at least malleable if you managed to somehow melt it.

Alice had tried to glare Sebille away too, but my fearless assistant stared her down and then asked the cranky ex-librarian if she'd like a cuppa.

So, as Sebille created magic in a teacup, her pointed ears perked so as not to miss a single word of the "turtle tale", Alice gave me the high points of her quest to Croakies.

"I told you, Naida, Tildy's in danger. I've taken her through time and across continents, trying to keep her safe. But that horrible woman keeps finding us."

Sebille placed a steaming teacup in front of Alice, earning a half-smile for her efforts.

"Who is this woman?" my courageous assistant asked.

Alice sighed her disgust at actually having to explain why she'd parked a five hundred pound dinosaur at Croakies. "I'll speak very slowly, shall I?"

Sebille's hands fisted and I was pretty sure her "Wicked Witch of the West" shoes were starting to smoke. I tugged on the flared sleeve of Sebille's neon green and hot pink checked dress, giving her a warning look when she scraped me with a glower of her own.

"Humor us, Alice," I said. "Amazingly, we've misplaced our universal spy glasses, so we aren't aware of your recent activities." Or non-recent. I hadn't actually heard from my old mentor since the day she skirted her responsibilities with a hop, skip, and ecstatic jump and left me in the lurch to learn how to become an artifact wrangler all by my lonesome.

But I'm not bitter.

No. Not me.

She sipped her tea. "This is very good," she told Sebille, surprise evident in her voice.

We waited while she sipped again. After she'd drained half her cup, she sat back and sighed. "Tildy is the last of her breed. A valuable and highly magical creature that had recently been safe in her little enclosure in a small zoo in the Caymans. Hidden in plain sight, if you will. But one day, a woman wandered into the zoo, looking for entertainment under the palm trees on a too-hot summer day. That woman did what no one else had done in over a hundred years. She recognized Tildy's magic."

"The Sorceress?" I guessed.

Alice nodded. "Most people don't understand the value of a magical tortoise. It's not well known even in magical circles."

"How did *you* know?" Sebille asked.

Amazingly, Alice didn't take offense at Sebille's question. "I did my senior work project at University on the ethical challenges of keeping magical creatures. I was something of an activist in my day." She sniffed. "I used the magical tortoise as the centerpiece of that thesis because they've been horribly mistreated over the centuries by science-minded magical knowledge seekers."

"Why?" I asked.

"Why? For the prodigious magical properties of their shells, yeah?" Alice cast what seemed to be a genuinely sad look on Tildy. "I fear that Tildy is the last magical tortoise in existence."

That was sad. It was really sad. We all stared at the massive bump in the bookstore. She stared back, her jaws moving over a lettuce leaf that was bigger than my head. Her eyes were kind and she seemed serene, despite the fact that Alice had, according to her, ripped her through time and continents. I blinked. "Wait, how in the Universe do you travel through time and across continents with something this big?"

Alice peered toward the small kitchen area of the store. "You don't, by chance, have something to nibble? Perhaps a nice scone? I'm sure you remember my delicious scones," she said to me, smiling.

I remembered them all right. I could have made good use of them a few times to beat monsters or giant gnomes senseless. "Um, we don't have any scones," I said, evading Alice's play for a compliment like a champ. I glanced at Sebille. "We might have a jelly donut?"

Sebille shook her head. "I ate the last one."

"Biscuit," Alice tried.

Sebille frowned. "We never eat biscuits…"

I shook my head. "She means cookies. I think I might have some upstairs. Would you?"

Sebille glared at me but turned on her heel and

clomped through the dividing door. She left it open, and I could hear her clomping loudly up the stairs.

I'd pay later for sending her on the errand. But I was afraid to leave her and Alice alone. Anything Sebille learned while I was gone, she might or might not share with me. To a sprite, knowledge was power, and they didn't always play well with others.

Plus, there's always the other problem. The two of them might kill each other while I'm putting frosted lemon drop cookies on a plate.

I looked at Alice. "You didn't answer my question," I reminded her.

"Well, isn't that obvious?"

Apparently not. "Humor me."

Alice motioned to Tildy. "I'll admit, she's not the most comfortable ride in the world. That shell's perfectly horrible on the bones. But she'll take you where you need to go in a blink."

I opened my mouth and snapped it closed again. I stared at Alice to see if she was joking.

She didn't appear to be.

I opened my mouth again. Words flew to my tongue and then bumped up against my teeth, tumbling down into a soup of unspent vocalizations as my mouth snapped closed again.

Alice's expression grew alarmed. "I say, are you all right, Naida? You're looking pale-ish."

I swallowed all the discarded words and dropped

into a chair next to Alice. "You're saying you rode the turtle?"

Alice looked into her empty teacup. Fortunately, she knew better than to ask me to make her more. We'd worked together for a few weeks before she'd skedaddled. She knew my tea tasted like the char from the bottom of a fire pit. And that was on a good day.

Sebille clomped loudly back down the steps. I gave her a smile as she came into the bookstore, holding a plate mounded with what looked like a dozen cookies. She'd cleaned out my entire stash!

The sprite returned my smile with a mean one of her own and I deflated, beaten like a bass drum in a rock band.

I shook it off as best I could. "Alice, you didn't ride that turtle down the road. You certainly didn't ride it over the ocean unless you have gills. How did you really get here?"

Alice plucked a cookie from the plate. "Don't be silly, Naida. One doesn't just plod down the lane on a magical tortoise."

"That's what I'm trying to say. I *know* one doesn't. What I'm asking is, what *does* one do?"

Her expression was filled with shock. "Are you saying you don't know about magical tortoises?"

Given that she'd just gotten done telling us that nobody knew much about magical tortoises, her question seemed unnecessary. I just stared at her.

She ate an entire lemon drop and reached for another, ignoring me.

"Alice?"

"Hopping hedgehog!" She shook her head. "A magical tortoise doesn't walk, Naida. It travels through magical portals of its own making, doesn't it?"

"Portals?" Sebille asked, dropping heavily into the last chair. "Spacial portals?"

Alice chewed the last bite of her second cookie, nodding. She scraped yellow crumbs from her lips and added, "and across time."

Sebille and I shared a long, shocked look.

Holy turtle toes! The car-sized dinosaur was a lumbering, lettuce-eating time machine!

Sebille bent closer to Tildy, peering carefully into the tortoise's calm, dark eyes. "So how do you work her? Is there a remote control or something?"

Alice harumphed. "Don't be daft. She's not a blooming telly. She's a living creature, i'nt she?"

I watched the two cats on the windowsill. They were both sitting upright, staring with fascination as a street sweeper crawled slowly past beyond the glass. Fenwald's long tail was scruffier than Mr. Wicked's, the fur patchy and rough. But it swung in time and rhythm that matched my beautiful boy's sleek gray one. They were two peas in a pod. It made me smile.

"Aren't they adorable, then?" Alice said.

I skimmed her a grin. "They haven't forgotten each other."

"Course not. It's only been a few months since I left after all."

Or three years. But who was I to quibble over thirty-three months? "Seems like just yesterday," I said, my lips twitching.

"Saucy thing," Alice said, bumping my shoulder with hers. But I heard the smile in her voice.

I turned my gaze to the elephant-sized problem in the room. "So...what do you need from me?"

Alice opened her mouth to respond but never got the chance.

The front door opened with a jangle of the bell. I frowned. I could have sworn I'd locked it behind Rustin and Lea. My pulse spiked. I couldn't have customers walking in to find a giant magical tortoise sitting in the middle of the store.

My panic quickly turned to shock when I saw who it was. "Oh!" I said, because...witty. "What are you doing here, Mr. Pudsnecker?" My mind slid to the envelope I'd hidden beneath a pile of books on Shakespeare's desk, and guilt ate a path through me. What if he was there to demand my reaction? I'd have to admit I'd been too afraid to read past the first few sentences.

I was a coward.

But Archibald Pudsnecker didn't seem to have come for me. He was busy glaring at Alice.

I barely had time to feel relief.

"Oy, Pudsy. How's things?" Alice asked with a smile.

Pudsy? I frowned, a fragment of a memory slicing its way from my subconscious and splatting on the floor as it unfolded fully in my mind.

Oy!

Pudsy!

3

YOU CAN'T PARK THE TURTLE HERE!

Well, that explained the familiar blue eyes and brown hair. I'd had the thought more than once that I'd seen the man somewhere before. But I'd never figured out where.

He'd clearly used some kind of magic to fog his features, making himself unnaturally forgettable.

"It's you!" I exclaimed, surprising the syrup out of Archibald Pudsnecker. His eyes went wide as I strode up to him with such contained violence he took a step back. My finger came up and I poked it at his bony, sweater-vest-clad chest. "You're Pudsy."

I'd had no idea the Void Keeper for the Société of Dire Magic was actually Pudsy from my early days at Croakies. Somehow he'd messed with my memories of him from those early days.

His blue eyes narrowed on Alice for a beat. "Only to her. The woman has no respect."

Alice blew a raspberry. "Can't have you taking yourself too seriously, can we, Pudsy?"

"No danger of that," he all but snarled out. "I'm pleased to see you finally answered my summons."

I blinked, lost. "Summons?" I looked at Alice. "Puds...um...Archie asked you to come? Why didn't you just tell me that?"

"Because my being here has nothing to do with any summons," she said, frowning in Archie's direction.

"You are a singularly difficult woman," Archie said, gritting his teeth.

"And you're an arrogant, self-important, azz..."

"Shut it, you two!" I ground out. "I want to talk about why you messed with my memories."

"What on earth are you talking about, Naida?" Alice demanded. "Have you gone daft?"

My glower never left Archie's face. "*He* knows what I'm talking about." I gave Archie's chest another poke to emphasize my accusation.

"It was a necessary precaution," the British rat squeaked.

"Why?"

He looked at Alice but found no help there. "Don't look at me, Pudsy. If you altered this girl's memories, you'll not get support from me."

Archie sighed. "Can we table that for the moment?" He pointed a long, well-manicured finger toward Tildy. "I need to know what that is doing here?"

"No, we cannot table it," I said. "I'm waiting for an answer to my question."

Archie stared at me for a beat and then asked, "Did you read the contents of that envelope I gave you?"

A long pause spun out between us. My eyes narrowed, causing his eyes to narrow. My lips compressed with irritation. Archie's lips compressed with irritation.

I panicked. He smiled, victory within his reach.

I gave in with consummate grace. "Fine! You win. But just know that I hate you with the heat of a billion, trillion burning suns."

Archie rubbed his hands together and grinned. "Well, that's that, then. Shall we have tea?"

Sebille cocked her head, bending in half to look the giant garbage disposal right in the eye. "What's your secret, turtle?"

Tildy chewed on, an enormous lettuce leaf slowly being dragged into her maw from the constant grinding motion.

Sebille reached out a hand.

Moving at the speed of...well...someone who wasn't her...Alice slapped the sprite's hand. "Don't touch."

"Ow!" Sebille surged to her feet, pale green energy spinning at her curved fingertips.

Alice rolled her eyes. "I'm only trying to save your life."

Sebille lifted a single, bright red eyebrow. "From that?" Derision ran from her in streams.

Alice shook her head. "Don't touch."

"She can't stay in the middle of my store," I said. "We have to move her into the artifact library."

We all eyed the people-sized door in question.

"Yeah, that's not going to work," Sebille said.

"No worries. Where's my bag?" Alice looked around, frowning. Her face suddenly cleared. "Ah. I left it in the loo."

She disappeared into said "loo" and returned with a leather backpack-style purse which she quickly proceeded to jam most of one arm and her head into. She rummaged around for a moment, mumbling incoherently. "Ah! There you are, you little beastie."

Alice's head emerged sporting a victorious smile, followed by her hand, which was clutching something.

"What is that?" I asked.

Alice held a tiny object out for me to see. The small rectangular thing was covered in tiny buttons carved onto a replica of a tortoise. It was smaller than the palm of the hand it was sitting on. "It's the key."

"Key?" Archie asked, his gaze narrowing.

"Yes," Alice nodded as if that explained everything. "Come along, girl," she said cheerfully. "We'll get you settled and then see about getting some supper."

Since Alice had already eaten all my cookies...at least the ones Sebille and I didn't eat...I hoped she wasn't thinking I was going to get her that supper. Between her and the hump-backed eating machine currently toddling toward the door, I'd need to take out a business loan just to keep myself in the black.

I didn't have to worry about that for long, though, because the dividing door between the library and the bookstore opened and a small creature with enormous blue eyes and a shock of light brown hair between large, pointed ears tore into the room. Wicked jumped down from his perch on the sill and bounced over to join his friend.

Holding Slimy against his tiny chest with one hand, Hobs stood in front of Alice, blinking up at her. His spidery fingers picked at the white cotton tunic he preferred. "Hello, ma'am."

Alice blinked in return, her generous form quivering with some strong emotion. "A hob..." she gasped, stumbling back a couple of steps. Her gaze tore to mine. "Naida! You're infested!"

I laughed. "No, I'm not. That's Hobs. He belongs..."

Quick as a wink, Alice grabbed the broom leaning against the wall and swung it at him. "Shoo, shoo!"

Hobs leaped over the broom, giggling as the stiff bristles swept across his oversized feet. It probably tickled. "Again!"

Um, sayeth the frog, his throat working overtime. *Is this...?*

Alice swung the broom so hard that, when she missed, she lost her balance and spun too far, bashing it against the door and barely catching herself against the wall.

"Hobs, why don't you and the cats go play in the back..." I said, trying to diffuse the situation.

Silly me.

"Meow!" Wicked said, his tail snapping. He trotted toward Tildy as Hobs' big blue eyes locked onto the tortoise, and he squealed. "Hobs of the Mountain!"

Apparently, he was no longer afraid of our new "artifact".

The meaning of his words oozed too slowly into my brain, and I was late moving. Too late. Unlike my cat, I wasn't adept at anticipating what the hobgoblin would do next.

In the blink of an eye, Hobs had leaped into the air, landing on the turtle's patchwork shell along with Wicked, who'd apparently intended to intercept his little friend but instead got caught up in the leap.

And, just like that, the whole gaggle disappeared in a tiny pop of displaced air.

Gone.

4

GONE, GONE, GONE, G...SLAP!

There was a beat of stunned silence.

I gave an uncertain laugh. "Okay, that's not funny, Alice. Bring them back."

Nothing. Still with the stunned silence.

Unease tickled along my spine. "Alice?"

Alice's mouth came open and she started to howl. It was an impressive sound, memorable for both its volume and its pitch.

And it made my blood curdle right inside my veins.

On the third howl, Archie said, "That will be quite enough." He stepped toward Alice and lifted a hand.

I made a grab for the hand, thinking he was going to smack her. I missed, but all he did was flick her on the button nose, making her enormous glasses wobble downward until they were perched on a micro-millimeter of pugnacious flesh.

The howls cut off as if sliced with a blade. Alice blinked in owlish surprise and sniffed, stabbing a finger against her enormous spectacles and glowering at Archie. "Of all the blood..."

He held up a long finger and she stopped mid-word.

"Not another word, Keeper. Histrionics will not return your turtle to the fold. We must think logically."

I took a deep breath and released it on a long sigh. "Whew! I really thought you were going to slap her."

Archie lowered bushy brown brows. "I'm British, Naida keeper. We prefer the razor edge of our tongues to physical violence."

"Oh, I don't know, I've tasted British food. It definitely did violence to my taste buds," Sebille murmured.

"She has a point." I made a *Sorry* face. Then I turned on Alice. "You can get them back, right? You have that..." I motioned toward her purse. "Clicker thing."

Alice started pacing. "She's gone. I can't believe she's gone."

The reality finally sank deep, and I suddenly found it hard to breathe. Wicked, Slimy, and Hobs were gone! Panic grabbed hold of my chest and yanked me forward. "Alice! Snap out of it. There has to be a way to find her."

"She's bloody gone. Gone, gone, gone, gone, g..."

Slap!

Archie and I twitched in surprise. Alice's mouth fell open, and she rubbed her red cheek. "Ouch."

Sebille nodded, looking pleased with herself. She glanced at a stunned Archie, shrugging. "I'm American. We have no trouble with a little well-placed violence if it's necessary."

He shuddered. "Neanderthals..."

I grabbed Alice's arms, barely resisting the urge to shake her. "How do we get them back?"

"I don't..." Her small eyes widened. "Oh, my, yes." She smiled. "The key!"

Hadn't I already said that? I rolled my eyes, feeling inadequate as I did. My eyes just didn't roll with the same effectiveness as Sebille's.

Alice reached into the pocket of her heavy wool skirt and pulled out the small rectangle, pressing a couple of buttons and then rubbing her thumb over the carved turtle's smooth head.

Nothing happened for a beat. I chewed on my bottom lip and twined my fingers together as stress ate through me. I was about to ask Alice if the key was working when the air in the center of the store started to thicken, turning opaque.

A strange scent swept through the room, like a combination of broken vegetation and manure, and then the carpet flattened in the shape of four enormous clawed feet.

I took a step back, pulling Sebille with me.

"Does that look right to you?" I asked Alice.

She ignored me, her expression calm.

A dark green blob splatted onto the carpet behind the impressions, steam wafting off of it along with a putrid stench.

"Oh my!" Archie said, covering his nose and stepping back.

Alice made a face. "She does that sometimes. Travel stresses her out."

A heartbeat later, Tildy popped into the spot in front of her steaming pile, enormous feet fitting right into the impressions that had showed up ahead of her.

She was alone. Sans riders.

My knees softened and I slid to the ground. "They're gone. How can they be gone? It's only been a minute since she disappeared."

Alice patted Tildy on the head.

The big turtle munched calmly on an enormous stem of widely serrated leaves that stuck out of both sides of her mouth. The leaves were dark green and didn't look like anything I'd ever seen before.

"It's only been a moment here," Alice explained. "But time might not have passed the same where they landed."

My heart beat against my ribs. "What? How much different could it be?" I demanded.

She shrugged. "Anywhere from a few minutes to a day or more."

Archie bent down and examined the leaf carefully. "I think we have a problem," he said, frowning.

"We have several problems," Sebille said. "All of them currently missing."

"Yes, yes, that's what I'm talking about." Archie pointed to the plant in Tildy's beaky mouth. "If I'm not mistaken, that's Cycadeoidea, a family within the order Bennettitales, which is an extinct group of seed plants. When this family of plants was prevalent, it was very popular with herbivores."

"So many big words," I complained. It made my head spin. The only part of his science-y statement that I really understood was the word "extinct". "When did it go extinct?" I asked.

His gaze slid to mine and held, filled with meaning I couldn't decipher except that I suspected I wouldn't like it. "They were believed extinct by the Cretaceous period." He continued to stare at me as if waiting for me to get it.

I stared back, my expression blank.

Finally, Alice said, "So that means..."

Archie nodded. "Our little friends are most likely running around somewhere in the middle of the Mesozoic Era. The Jurassic Period. Otherwise known as the Age of Reptiles."

Ring around the Reptile!

Wicked, Slimy, and Hobs were dancing with the dinosaurs!

I dropped my head into my hands, tears burning my eyes. "Dinosaurs. There's no way they'll survive that. Wicked will try to protect them all and get stomped or worse. Poor Slimy is vastly under-equipped to deal with reptiles a thousand times his size. And Hobs..." A sob worked its way up my throat. "He's a dead hobgoblin walking. No way will he stay out of trouble. And dinosaurs are trouble magnified fifty million times."

"On the bright side," the sprite said in a weak attempt to cheer me up. "The little guy will really enjoy it when they start batting him around. For a while..." She bit her bottom lip as she reached the exact spot in Despair Junction where I'd landed. "They're toast."

Another sob ripped through me.

"Well," Alice said, much too cheerfully. "I'm up for an adventure. How about you, Pudsy?"

Archie sighed, dropping into a chair. He looked a decade older than he had when he'd come through my door.

Imagine how quickly I was aging. I *lived* at Croakies.

"I don't see that we have any choice. Naida can't lose all her friends."

My head came up as my brain finally wrapped

around the fact that they were discussing a trip back in time to save the kids. My eyes widened. "Are you serious? You'd travel back millions of years to save them?"

"Of course," Alice said, shrugging.

Archie gave me a fond smile. "Certainly, dear girl. I only wonder that you're surprised."

Sebille suddenly landed next to me on the dusty carpet, a frown on her freckled face.

"What?" I asked.

She slowly turned her gaze to me. "They have to be all right, Naida."

The terrifying reality had just slammed into her. I reached to squeeze her hand. "They will be. We're going to make sure of it."

If only I believed my own words.

5

JUST ANOTHER OGRE ON A TREADMILL

How does one pack for the Jurassic period? I had no idea. I stared down at the clothes I'd thrown over my bed and then eyed the single backpack Alice had told me I could bring. It wasn't much. And when I added food and bottles of water, I would only really have room for a pair of underwear and some socks.

I sighed. That wouldn't do. True, I probably wouldn't need a business suit or a dressy dress in the Jurassic era, but I was pretty sure it was a steamy time in history. Hot enough to boil an egg on a Cyclopsidea leaf...or whatever that stupid thing had been called. I was going to sweat. A lot. I didn't want to go around smelling like an ogre on a treadmill the whole time.

I grabbed my deodorant, throwing it into the bag. Just to be on the safe side, I grabbed two more sticks of deodorant and threw those in too. A girl could never have too much deodorant when running for her life in the primordial jungle.

That gave me another thought. Sunscreen. I had fair skin. I burned easily. Which meant that I'd probably look like a boiled lobster within an hour if we happened to land someplace sunny.

Maybe we'd land at night.

The thought gave me comfort until I thought about all the really scary stuff that could hide in the darkness during the Jurassic period.

Ugh!

I grabbed my biggest flashlight and slipped that into the bag. And some extra batteries.

Mosquitoes! I hated mosquitoes. Really, I hated bugs of all kinds. Especially the biting kind. I grabbed bug repellent and then started wondering how big a Jurassic era mosquito would be.

I felt faint at the picture my mind conjured up.

Buzzing bug butts!

I threw in another can of repellent.

Eyeing the bag, I grimaced. I tugged it off the bed by one strap and groaned under the weight. It was already a hundred pounds, and I hadn't added the food and water yet.

Le sigh.

"Helloo!" The door to my apartment opened and Alice stuck her head inside, her beady gaze sliding around the room as she stepped over the threshold. "My heavens! This looks a bit different, yeah?"

I didn't feel like making small talk. "I can't get everything I need into one bag. What are you taking?" I asked the former Keeper.

She ran her hands over her chubby form, which was covered in a pair of baggy, stretchy pants, a long-sleeved tee-shirt that said *Jungle Bunny* on the front, and a canvas vest that had more pockets than twelve pairs of cargo pants. "Everything I need is in this vest."

I eyed the aforementioned pockets, noting that most of them bulged suspiciously. "Water?"

She pulled out a tiny canister thing. "A personal water purifier straw."

I felt my eyes go round. "Say what?"

Alice shook her head, disgusted by my ignorance. "Haven't you ever spent time in the wild?"

"Not unless you call Enchanted Park the wild," I admitted.

She clucked her tongue. "Here, take this one. I have spares."

I took the straw and eyed it carefully. "This will work with a water bottle?"

She snorted. "No water bottles. You couldn't possibly carry enough of them to suit. That straw will suffice."

I shrugged. "I'll take your word on that," I said.

"That *would* be a first," Alice grumbled beneath her breath.

I frowned. "So, I was thinking I'd bring canned food because it doesn't need to be refrigerated." I grinned, proud of my creative thinking. Imagine my surprise when she laughed outright. A real belly laugh. One that doubled her over so deeply that some of the stuff fell out of her vest pockets.

She grabbed one of the fallen items and held it up in front of me. "This..." she hiccupped another laugh. "This is what you'll be bringing."

I squinted at the tiny, foil-wrapped item. "You got a taco in that thing?" I asked.

She glowered. Apparently, she no longer found me funny. "No cans, no fresh food, nothing that takes up any room or could spoil in temperatures that will be well over a hundred degrees."

I grimaced. "Well, over a hun..." I was going to need more deodorant.

She slipped the foil thingie back into a vest pocket. "Protein bars without any chocolate or frosting of any kind. Meat jerky. Dried fruit if you insist. Nuts. That's all."

I shrugged. "In other words, only stuff that tastes like a demon's backside?"

"Precisely."

"I'm guessing that means no hairdryer?"

Laughing hysterically at some joke only she understood, Alice turned and headed out of the apartment, throwing a final instruction over her shoulder as she left. "We're leaving in fifteen minutes."

Yikes! I didn't have any of the food items she'd just told me I'd need. I had to run to the store and there was no time.

Sebille came through the door, a zip lock bag in her hands. "Here." She handed it to me.

"What's this?" I asked, peering inside.

"The only thing between you and certain death."

I pulled out several of the foil-wrapped things and some other stuff that fit into Alice's too-narrow food parameters. "Where'd you get all this?"

"I ran to the store."

Thank the goddess, somebody had been thinking ahead. "Thank you!" I told her, my tone sincere. "You saved my life."

"I know. Don't get so excited. It's an almost daily occurrence."

"Har." I eyed her outfit, finding it strangely compelling. While I was used to seeing her in below-the-knee-length dresses, striped socks, and shiny red Wicked Witch of the West shoes, The baggy camo-themed capris with green and white striped socks and bright red sneakers were strangely similar. Only the plain, brown t-shirt ruined the "Sebille" effect.

My assistant plopped onto the bed next to my bag, her skinny butt pressing my pretty new scoop-necked top into the comforter.

I pointed to it. "You're, uh, sitting on my clothes."

Sebille rolled her eyes. "You're not taking any of those."

I blinked. "I'm not?"

She shook her head. "Of course not. Have you never been to the jungle before?"

"Um, let's see..." I pretended to think about it, tapping my lips with my finger. I shook my head. "Nope."

She rolled her eyes again. If she wasn't careful, they were going to get stuck that way someday. "This is a quick in and out mission. If we're not out of there within a few hours, we're all going to die horrific deaths."

I swallowed hard, dropping onto the bed next to her. "Gee, when you put it that way, it takes all the fun out of it."

"Heh." She grabbed two tank tops, one bra, and an extra pair of underwear and stuffed them into the backpack. "There, you're done."

I stared at the pathetic collection in the pack, feeling my stomach twist with alarm. "But..."

Sebille patted me on the back, hard enough to almost throw me off the bed. "Suck it up, buttercup. We're going into the jungle during the Jurassic era. We'll be lucky if a T-Rex doesn't chomp us like movie popcorn the minute we land. Believe me when I say that your fashion choices are the least of your worries."

I watched Sebille stomp through the door, my mouth hanging open.

Whatever you might say about my assistant, the sprite, she definitely didn't pull any punches.

Working my jaw to make sure it was still attached after Sebille's verbal takedown punch, I pushed to my feet. I grabbed another pair of underwear and stuffed them into the pack, sticking my tongue out at the closed door.

Yeah. I know, maturity, thy name is Naida.

Whatever.

———

Oliver was blinking at me from Slimy's tank. There were live crickets hopping all around him and fresh water filling Slimy's little pool to the brim. Fenwald was asleep in a stripe of sun that painted the carpet. I noticed Wicked's food and water bowls were full on the floor of the tea area.

Alice noticed me frowning and said, "They'll be fine here. We'll be back in the blink of an eye."

I knew she was right. They'd both be good for several days with the amount of food and water Alice had left, and if we were gone longer than that, one of our friends would be breaking down Croakies' door to see what had happened to us.

The thought soured my stomach.

We had to find Wicked, Hobs, and Slimy and get everybody safely back.

We just had to.

Archie was standing in the middle of the store staring at Tildy. I slouched across the room, all my weight on my heels as the backpack drove me into the floorboards. I was already sweating and my shoulders ached from the weight of the thing.

The void sorcerer was wearing his black robes and carried nothing that I could see. Sebille was leaning against the short wall next to the tea area, sipping from a steaming cup. I stared longingly at the cup, wishing I could have some. I must have drooled a little bit because Sebille frowned at me.

"You want tea?"

I forced myself to shake my head, though it nearly made me whimper. The truth was that I'd love a cuppa, but I was pretty sure there were no porta-potties in the jungle, and tea went right through me. My goal was to hold everything in until we got home.

That thought had been the only thing keeping me from jamming a roll of TP into my backpack. That, and the fact that there wasn't an inch of space left in the thing.

The backpack shifted as I tried to make my nonchalant way across the store to Alice, who was frowning over some kind of map, turning the turtle key around and around in her fingers.

She glanced up as I approached, eyeing me with a narrowed gaze. She slowly tipped her head to match the slant of my shoulders. "Why are you tilting like the Tower of Pisa?"

I shifted to the other foot and the backpack resettled, its weight slamming onto my other side and nearly taking me down to the floor.

Alice gave a long-suffering sigh. "Turn around."

I backed away from her. "Why?"

She pointed a finger toward the carpet and circled it. "Turn."

I expelled air and turned.

She unzipped the pack and rummaged around in it with such force it jerked me from side to side. Behind me, things clanged to the ground.

I tried to turn my head. "Hey!"

The pack became blissfully lighter. "I need all that stuff."

"No, you don't. We're not going to be there long enough to need it." Her tone was unhappy. I couldn't help remembering Sebille's statement about getting in and out or dying.

"There." Alice rezipped the bag and patted it. "Good to go."

I spun to find my deodorant, flashlight, batteries, bug spray, and the extra pair of underwear and bra that I'd stuffed into the bag, strewn about the floor. "I need that stuff!" I objected, angry heat climbing to my face.

"The pack's too heavy," Alice argued.

"It's not your business if I carry a heavy pack," I yelled.

"Isn't it?" she yelled back. "What if we need to run from something? A highly likely event, I can assure you. One of us might get eaten trying to save you when you lag behind."

My mouth opened and then closed. She had a point.

"We need to go," Archie said, his bushy gray-brown brows lowering. "Enough of this bickering."

There was tension in the lines of his distinguished face. With a start, I realized the sorcerer was scared. It was no wonder since he didn't appear to be bringing so much as a single piece of jerky along with him.

I shrugged the pack higher on my shoulders and stepped toward the tortoise. "How does this work?" I asked the air beside Alice's head since I was too ticked to look her in the eye.

"We can't all get on Tildy. The poor girl couldn't carry this much weight. So we'll stand two on each side and simply touch the edge of her shell."

As we moved closer, she added, "Don't touch the scute, whatever you do. Each section on her shell represents a certain time or place. I must touch the right ones in the right order to get us exactly where we need to go."

I tried to remember what Hobs had touched when he'd landed on Tildy's shell, but it had happened too quickly. And Wicked had landed about the same time. The combination of what his paws and Hobs' feet and hands touched must have been what sent them to the Jurassic era. Alice would have to touch the sections of the shell in exactly the same way and order for us to arrive where, and when, they had.

I suddenly realized how difficult our journey was going to be. If Alice was off by even a tiny bit, we might land in the wrong spot, maybe hundreds of miles away, or even the wrong era.

My heart started to pound and my palms to sweat.

I stepped up to Tildy beside Alice. Sebille and Archie arranged themselves on the opposite side. We all stared expectantly at Alice as she studied the key, brow furrowed.

After a moment, she said. "Here we go."

She leaned down and touched a pink section at the front of the shell with her left hand while instructing Sebille to place her palm over the green one just in front of the tortoise's tail. Alice looked at Archie. "Pudsy, place your right palm on the chartreuse section and your left on the purple, taking care to touch them both at the same time."

He did as he was instructed.

Alice looked at me. "When I say go, place a hand

on the dark green section and don't lift it no matter what."

I felt my eyes go wide. That sounded really dire. "Why didn't you tell anybody else that?" Had she given me the most important part? Or did she think I was such a screwup I needed extra instruction?

Alice ignored me. She glanced at Tildy's head, which moved slightly under the impetus of her chewing. Did the critter never stop eating? "Okay, here we go. On three."

I tensed, my hand hovering over my assigned section.

"One..."

My nose itched.

"Two..."

It itched sooooo bad. I lifted a finger of my free hand and scratched it.

"Three!"

I slammed my hand down. The backpack shifted violently from the movement, along with the action of me dropping the hand that I'd been using to scratch. The pack slammed sideways, falling off my shoulder and smacking Alice's hip.

She yowled in pain. Something dropped to the ground just as the air began to swirl. Pink and pale green sparkles danced around us. The floor disappeared, and we were suddenly shooting through a long, black tunnel that smelled like grass and leaves and other growing things.

I tried to turn my head to see what everyone else was doing, but I couldn't move. I was locked into place, my body vibrating as if I stood atop a washing machine. All I could do was watch the bright green and blue ending point of the tunnel shoot inexorably toward me.

I suddenly didn't want to land there.

Heat pulsed from our destination. Moist, cloying heat. It brought with it the nearly overwhelming stench of reptile.

Really big reptile.

As we finally shot from the end of the tunnel, an enormous roar shook the air around us. The terrifying sound followed us as we shot like a rocket toward the huge, blue body far below. The primitive bellow vibrated the air, covering me in icy dread. If there had been any possible way to do it, I would have turned around and Fred-Flinstoned it right back into that tunnel.

But we were locked and loaded, plummeting toward my worst nightmare.

I could still hear the blood-chilling roar as I hit the lukewarm water of an enormous lake and sank like a prehistoric stone.

6

JINXED JURASSIC STYLE!

The water closed over me, a warm, chunky wash that slid across my skin with spidery fingers. I was so disoriented for a moment I just let myself sink, my stunned ears barely noticing the distant wails and strange growls reverberating through the lake.

The water washed over me in a constant state of churn, slashing against my body rather than flowing. I finally opened my eyes as my brain deciphered what the churning water meant.

I found myself staring into a pair of slitted, hostile eyes in a relatively small head. The body behind the head was turtle-like. It had paddles for legs and a short tail. But the thing's neck was much too long for it to be a turtle. It reminded me of pictures I'd seen of the Loch Ness monster.

We stared at each other for a beat, me too afraid

to move and the thing in front of me seemingly trying to figure out what I was. Then the mouth opened, and I jolted backward in stark terror. Thin, needle-like teeth decorated the upper and lower jaws, deadly enough to rip the flesh right off my quivering frame.

I was about to become dinner.

A dark shape exploded into view from the left and rammed into Nessie's distant cousin, sending her spiraling off into the cloudy water.

Predator, meet apex predator.

Gulp! I sprang into movement, spurred by sheer terror.

My lungs burned, desperately in need of air, and I needed to move or I was going to end up somebody's early bird dinner special. Unfortunately, all those donuts and tacos I favored had fattened me up nicely, making me an enticing main course.

I kicked hard, my arms pressing against the churning liquid, and rose maybe a foot in the water.

A long, eel-like fish with massive teeth swam past, giving me only a cursory glance as it high-tailed it away from the watery battle going on behind me.

I kicked harder, trying to propel myself upward and finding it nearly impossible to rise.

My chest screamed and panic was a living thing in my chest.

I didn't want to drown in that prehistoric lake. I had things I needed to do. Friends to save.

Wicked, Slimy, Hobs. Thinking of them tightened my chest even more.

And then there were my friends who'd risked almost certain death to join me in our ill-fated mission to the prehistoric jungle.

I kicked for all I was worth. Gaining another foot. Something was holding me down, dragging against me as I tried to swim.

I wasn't going to make it.

The water darkened and I cast a frantic glance around, looking for the danger that was literally shadowing me.

Something massive moved slowly and steadily past overhead. Once it passed, a forest of velvety vegetation engulfed me, swayed by its passage.

I had an instinctive fear of weeds in deep water. My entire body shuddered.

Renewing my struggle to rise to the top, I kicked as hard as my quickly numbing legs would allow. I was getting weak from lack of air.

I was going to die.

Something slammed into me, the force shoving me an impossible distance through the chunky water. Without warning, I felt the burn of enormous teeth scraping against my back.

Adrenaline poured through me, giving me a gust of renewed energy. I fought against the pull of the monster that had clamped its terrifying teeth around my backpack. Literally fighting for my life.

But my strength was no match for the monster's, and I began to feel myself being pulled backward.

My pulse thundered in my ears. A sob built in my throat. I didn't want to die.

Something ripped, and the pressure released with an abruptness that shot me forward. Kicking hard, I glided through the churning water, propelled by a tsunami of adrenaline. I broke the surface on a gasp and a splutter. My feet touched silty ground and I stumbled forward, hands grasping for me and pulling me from the water.

Familiar voices chewed the air around me. I was too busy sucking sweet air into my lungs to concentrate on them. It had been the backpack. That was what had been dragging me down. But in the end, it had saved my life.

I coughed and coughed, nasty tasting water spewing from between my lips. Someone tugged me onto my side as I retched and retched until I had nothing left inside me to throw up.

I lay there panting, and listened to my friends argue. All of them talking at once.

I finally rolled to my back and focused on the words.

"...trapped! What are we supposed to do now?" That was Archie.

"I can't believe you dropped the key!" That was

the sprite. I was used to her angry voice. But what I was hearing was closer to desperation than anger.

"It wasn't my fault," Alice said, sounding scared and angry. "That stupid backpack knocked it out of my pocket."

I blinked as they all turned to look at me, feeling guilty. "Um. Sorry?" My voice was hoarse, and using it made me cough again.

Luckily for me, that bought me a pity allowance. Their hostile stares slid away.

When I could talk again, I said. "What's the big deal? We'll just keep touching sections on Tildy's shell until we get someplace or sometime close to home."

They all expelled air, staring into the pond with hard eyes. The three of them were dripping wet too, so I guessed I wasn't the only one who'd dropped into the drink when we arrived.

"I'm afraid it won't be that easy," Archie finally said, turning his familiar blue gaze to me.

"Why?" I pushed to a sitting position in the wet sand. My arms felt like rubber and barely managed to shove me upright.

Alice fixed me with a haunted look. "Because Tildy disappeared when we landed. She's gone. And she took our only hope of returning home with her."

I expelled a long, frustrated breath. *Dinosaur dangles*!

We were jinxed Jurassic style!

If we didn't have bad luck, we'd have no luck at all.

—

I pushed through the broken vegetation behind Sebille, jerking my head back as yet another wide, wet leaf slapped the air where my face had been. Warm droplets of water sprayed my sweat-drenched skin. Despite the pique driving the slap, it felt good. I glowered at the back of the sprite's fire-red head. "It's not my fault we're stuck here," I told her for about the dozenth time.

I didn't need to see her face to know she was rolling her eyes at me. Her disgust stiffened every line of her posture and showed in the relentless way she kept slapping me with wet vegetation.

"I tried to call her back," I whined. "Alice tried too. She's gone, Sebille. Out of this time or dimension. I did everything I could..." Since Tildy was technically an artifact, albeit an unregistered one, my Keeper magic should have called her to me. If she was close enough to respond.

Sebille's rigid posture only stiffened more. I read the accusation in her ramrod carriage. If my stupid backpack hadn't knocked Tildy's clicker from Alice's pocket, we wouldn't currently be stranded in the Jurassic era.

I sighed. Technically, she was right. But the back-pack sliding hadn't been my fault. Had it?

I shoved away guilty thoughts of overstuffing the pack against the advice of everyone in my party. Instead, I focused on creating a defense for my actions.

The effort involved in that exercise was substantial.

My thoughts locked into self-justification in the face of so much hostility, I almost missed it when she stopped short. Throwing on the brakes, I barely kept from slamming into Sebille's narrow, rigid back. From the front of the line, Archie said, "The trail ends here."

We'd been lucky enough to find a broken trail of small feet and tiny paws leading from the clearing by the lake. The prints seemed to verify that we'd prob-ably landed in the right spot.

Archie was announcing that he'd lost the kids' tracks. A disturbing though predictable outcome. But not a happy one.

No easy task given the vast amount of vegetation and the thousands of massive prints churning up the dirt.

Our heads swiveled to take in the area, which included a lot of trees and plants and an abundance of ridiculously steamy air. Pretty much like all the other areas we'd passed through. Though, if I'd been given the choice of traipsing through the jungle or taking another swim in the prehistoric pond, I'd choose the jungle hands down.

I couldn't help wondering if that stupid fish dinosaur had swallowed my deodorant and bug spray. Maybe the flashlight had come on as he swallowed, and he was swimming around in that murky water with a tracking beacon shining from his ugly face. *Here I am even bigger dinosaur fish. Come and eat me!*

The thought made me feel a tiny bit better about losing my deodorant.

Slapping at a bug that was big enough to punch me back, I scratched mindlessly at the nostril-sized red spot it left in my flesh.

I was sick of being a walking sippy cup for Jurassic-sized bugs.

Knock, knock. Who's there?

Door to door blood delivery service for bugs the size of your head.

What's the punch line?

My fist.

Shaking off my weird musings, which I'd decided were the ugly result of the recent lack of oxygen, coupled with having my brain boiled in the hot wet air of the jungle, and maybe severe blood loss from the 747-sized mosquitoes, I focused on Archie. "What does that mean?"

"I'm not sure." His expression looked grim.

A fresh wave of fear sliced through me. Judging

by Archie's face, he didn't believe it had been Wicked's, Hobs', and Slimy's choice to disappear from the path. Which meant...

A strident cry impaled the sky above. We all cranked our heads up to view the terrifying spectacle of three enormous bird dinosaurs circling beneath a leaden gray sky like vultures.

I swallowed hard as bile tried to rise into my throat.

"Pterodactyls," Archie said, looking grim. "We should..."

The sky growled long and low. Spears of silvery lightning stabbed toward the ground, illuminating the dense bank of clouds from within.

"...find shelter," Archie finished as the sky opened up and dumped a dense blanket of water onto our heads. The rain fell in a nearly solid silver curtain that pounded painfully against my skin and stole the world away. The sheer amount of falling liquid was blinding.

One of those sharp-faced carnivorous flying dinosaurs could swoop down from the sky and grab me before I even knew it was there.

Our only hope was if they were as discombobulated by the torrential rain as we were.

Something grabbed my arm and tugged. Instinctive panic flooded me and I gave a terrified little scream, my fingers ripped at the object wrapped around me like a bony vise.

It took my panicked mind a minute to realize what was under my fingers.

Human skin. Something wide and dark green was thrust against my chest. I looked down to find Sebille's bony hand pressing a large leaf toward me.

I grabbed it and used it to keep the rain off my head. I could see a little better, though it took me a beat to realize my posse had moved out. I hurried after them, my sneakers splashing wetly through a trail of quickly-growing mud puddles.

The water was over my ankles and a solid river rushing past us down the narrow path by the time we found a deep indentation in the rock. The painful, water-based beating was sliced off at the cave's wide entrance.

I groaned in relief, lowering my leafy umbrella and swiping a stream of water out of my eyes as I looked around. "They're serious about their rain-storms here," I muttered.

Sebille wrung out one of her braids. "I just want to be the first to say that I hate the Jurassic era."

"Amen and amen," I agreed.

Archie collapsed onto a flattish rock with a weary sigh. "We'll rest here until morning."

I frowned at the still prodigious downpour beyond the cave opening. "Hopefully, this will be gone by then."

Archie didn't say anything, but his lips compressed into a firm, straight line.

"What?" I asked, narrowing my gaze on him.

"Nothing." He shook his head. "We need to rest and eat and get warm."

A shushing sound drew my gaze to the center of the space. Alice briskly rubbed something together over a pile of sticks. "We'll need a fire."

Archie frowned. "Do you think that's wise? We don't want to draw the attention of any predators."

I blinked. "Do you think there are some nearby?" Yes, it was a stupid question, but my muscles contracted into hard knots and I shuddered at the thought of being attacked by any of the monstrosities we'd witnessed during our trek through the jungle.

I'd been fascinated by the small group of Brachiosaurus we'd passed not long after we started off. The enormous dinosaurs seemed like gentle giants, and they made soft cooing sounds to each other as they munched leaves like the one Tildy had brought back and moved slowly through the trees.

We'd seen smaller, faster dinos too. And had almost been eaten by a giant alligator near the water hole where we'd landed. Archie had told me it was a Deinosuchus.

He was right. It definitely did suck.

Besides, I didn't really care what its name was. An alligator by any other name is definitely not a rose.

Sebille snorted. "Everything in this era is a predator."

"Well, technically..." Archie began.

Sebille and I shared a look as he started off on what would no doubt be a long lecture on dinosaur types and practices.

He probably didn't even notice when we wandered deeper into the cave looking for more sticks for the fire.

7

I SAY, YOU'RE VERY STRONG AREN'T YOU, PUDSY?

The rain formed constant white noise as we slept. It was like a drug, combining with the stress and weariness of the previous day to send me into a deep, restless sleep. Thunder rolled through my dreams, lit by the occasional flare of silver light from beyond the opening.

The torrential downpours filtered into my dreams, transforming into murky water and helpless terror. In my dream, I thrashed, fighting to break free of the horrifying presence yanking me down. And finally, when a terrible roar yanked me from sleep and sent me jolting upright from my hard, bumpy bed on the floor, I knew it was more exhausting to sleep than it would be to remain awake.

I brushed sweat from my face with the sleeve of my shirt, catching a sour whiff of myself and grimacing. My worst fears were realized. I was in dire need of deodorant and a fresh change of clothes.

Dang water monster. I hoped the contents of my backpack gave him rampant diarrhea.

The dying fire cast soft ripples of weak light over the walls, lighting only a circular area about eight feet in diameter.

My three traveling companions were still asleep. I stared at their unmoving, seemingly peaceful forms and nurtured a spike of jealousy.

Archie lay on his back, mouth parted and thin, whispery snores emerging from between his lips. His elegant fingers, covered in dirt but still somehow keeping it classy, twitched on his belly where they lay.

Alice's snores were tiny little warbles, like the sound of a mother bird soothing her hatchlings.

Sebille belted out a sound that was right at home in the Jurassic Jungle. A cross between a velociraptor's screech and a whistle, it emerged through lips that were slack in sleep. A thin trail of drool slid from the corner of her mouth and trailed down her cheek.

I shook my head, remembering that snore all too clearly from our weeks of sharing my apartment. The memory was a waking nightmare that made me shudder.

I yawned widely and pushed to my feet, groaning as my entire body clenched in a painful muscle spasm. *Holy horned reptiles!* I wasn't even thirty yet and I already felt a hundred years old. My job was going to kill me well before my time.

When the pain had softened from all-encompassing agony to general misery, I moved toward the mouth of the cave, standing just inside and watching in fascination as rain fell from the sky in a dense, impenetrable blanket.

The water was an inch deep on the ground, leaching into the cave in glossy fingers before easing backward to rejoin the overflow outside and rush downward, away from where I stood.

I couldn't see the area around the cave, but I remembered having the sense of climbing as we'd approached the shelter. Hopefully, if the giant lake we'd landed in decided to flood, we'd be safe in our little hidey-hole on the hill.

Any reassurance that thought gave me was quickly dashed as I remembered why we'd come. *Mr. Wicked...*

Sadness softened my knees, and I had to lean against the rocky wall or risk falling on my face in the dirt. Tears burned my eyes.

Were Wicked, Slimy, and Hobs someplace safe? What if they hadn't found shelter? And if they had, was it high enough to save them if the area flooded?

My empty stomach twisted in alarm, then rumbled, hunger making itself known despite the fear burning there. Wrapping my arms around my middle, I let the tears fall. All my food was gone, digesting in the enormous belly of the Loch Ness monster lookalike swimming around the distant lake. I couldn't take food from the others. We didn't know how long we were going to be stuck there. They'd need everything they had and more.

My mouth was dry too. I lamented the loss of the water bottles I'd stuck into my pack in a moment of proud rebellion and then had quickly regretted as I slipped the straps of the twelve-hundred-pound pack over my wimpy, soft-muscled shoulders.

I eyed the rain, a thought percolating through my brain.

We were over a hundred million years in the past. There was no such thing as air pollution in the Jurassic era, right?

Acid rain? Unlikely.

Hmm.

I glanced back at my companions, finding them still deeply asleep, and then made the decision.

I stuck my head out and tipped my chin up, opening my mouth and sticking out my tongue to capture the water raining down from above.

It hit my tongue in a warm but not unpleasant wash. I gulped it gratefully.

Thump.

I jerked at the muffled sound, swallowing the water wrong and choking. I coughed for a full minute, most of the sound lost beneath the roar of the rain.

I listened for a minute, hearing nothing but the rain, and then shrugged. It must have been thunder. I held my hands out to catch the water and then grimaced. My hands were filthy. I scrubbed them under the fall of water, trying to get them clean.

Thump!

The ground shook under a slight vibration.

I went very still.

Thump!

Dirt sifted down from above, peppering my head and shoulders. I sneezed and then slapped a hand over my face, my eyes riveted to the curtain of water and my heart doing the rhumba against my ribs.

Thump!

Was it getting louder?

Thump!

The ground shook, small rocks slipped down the walls and pinged against my sneakers.

Thump! Thump! Thump!

I backpedaled, my eyes wide, and bumped up against Sebille.

She came awake with a throat-searing snort and jerked upright. "Huh?" The sprite blinked slowly, looking like she didn't know where she was. Then her expression cleared and turned sour. "Oh." She glowered up at me. "What in the name of the goddess's favorite deodorant are you doing, Naida?"

I winced. She would have to mention deodorant. Probably a subliminal reaction to my stench. I pointed to the opening. "There's something out there." To my everlasting shame, my finger shook.

She pushed to her feet and shoved her long, fiery hair off her face. It was odd to see Sebille's waist-length hair loose. She almost always wore it in one or two braids. "Something's coming this way?" she asked, her voice slightly deeper than usual from sleep.

"It sounded like it was getting closer."

We both stood there for a long moment, hearing nothing but rain. And the occasional *Whir, wisp, wisp, wisp* of Archie's snoring.

Some of the tension leached from our muscles and Sebille rolled her eyes, an unusual relief in the action. "Drama Mama," she accused.

I happily accepted the accusation, glad to be wrong. "Heh. Yeah, I guess I'm a nervous Nelly."

Sebille grinned with me.

The curtain of rain split apart and a giant head shot through.

Sebille and I jumped, squealing with alarm. We slammed together as we both tried to run in opposite directions.

Rather than shove me away as she normally would, Sebille wrapped her skinny arms around me and locked me in a bony vise, quivering like a baby bird and squeaking like a mouse.

The massive jaw opened and an unimaginable sound exploded from it in a roar that blew Sebille and me to the back of the cave.

The roar ended and Sebille squeaked again, her bony knees clanking together. Her grip on my chest was terrifying, compressing my lungs until I couldn't breathe.

Archie sat bolt upright, his blue eyes blinking rapidly. He stared at the giantnormous head in the opening and the blinking slowed. "Tyrannosaurus Rex," he said, tilting his head. "Fascinating."

The head shifted. The rain split wider as a massive chest and two ridiculously small arms came through.

Sebille squeaked again and clutched me tighter.

I sucked air but not enough of it filtered into my chest. "I can't...breathe," I gasped.

The monstrous reptile stopped again, swung its massive head up, and bellowed another roar. A wild, unidentifiable stench pressed Sebille and me against the wall, plastering the rock behind us in dual hair auras, one bright red and one dark brown.

Archie all but levitated to his feet. He sidled sideways and nudged Alice with a foot. "Get up!"

I couldn't believe she was still sleeping through all the roaring and knee-knocking and the sound of too little air wheezing in and out of my lungs.

Alice moved away from Archie's foot with a mumbled sigh and then settled back to sleep.

"How can she sleep through this?" Sebille asked in a too-high voice.

Archie nudged her a little harder. "Alice! Get. Up!"

The former keeper opened her eyes and yawned, stretching her arms over her head. "Is it morning already?" She pushed to a seated position and shoved her messy brown curls away from her face, blinking. Her hands skimmed the nearby dirt looking for her coke bottle glasses. "I know I left them here somewhere...ah, there they are!"

Archie motioned to us. "Come here, girls."

Sebille clutched me harder and shook her head, her eyes nearly popping out of her head.

I tried to shuffle toward Archie. He probably had a good idea of how to get us out of there.

Sebille dug her toes in and held on. "I'm not moving an inch closer to that...that..."

Alice frowned. "What, what?"

Archie grabbed Alice under the arms and yanked her to her feet.

Her squeal ended in a girlish giggle. "Oh! I say. You're very strong aren't you, Pudsy?"

Archie started backing toward us, pulling Alice with him. "Be quiet," he told Alice. "Don't make any sudden moves."

She giggled again, batting her eyelashes at him. "Trying to get me alone," she said, smacking him on the chest. "Dirty boy."

Archie grunted. "Stop talking!" he said in a stern undertone.

Alice sighed. "You know I'm a sucker for an alpha male, Puds..."

ROAR!!!!!

Alice's head shot up and her hair blew away from her face. Her glasses elevated off her nose and started to blow away but she slammed a finger to the bridge before they could achieve liftoff, smashing them back onto her face.

She stared at the terrifying apparition in the opening for a beat. Then her mouth came open and she let loose a scream that scraped dust from the rocks and made the T-Rex rear back in surprise.

A beat of silence followed, during which the Rex and Alice faced off, trying to determine which of them was the true apex.

It was no contest. The only thing Alice was apex at was creating pastries that could be used as clubs.

I suddenly wished for a few of her scones. Maybe we could feed them to the T-Rex and all his teeth would break from chewing them.

As predicted, Alice lost the stare down.

Two things happened at once.

Archie lifted his hands, sending magic tingling along my skin.

And the train-sized monster in the doorway burst into the cave and thundered toward us.

8

A-VOID THIS!

We all screamed and cowered toward the ground as the massive jaws opened and snapped around us. Even as I shrieked in uncontrollable terror, I waited for the agony of those impossibly huge teeth ripping me in half.

The teeth did indeed slice through the air where we stood.

Except we were no longer fully there.

The mouth closed harmlessly over the shadows of our disappearing forms and then faded away, leaving us in a bubble of lightless nothing.

As the last of our horrified shrieking died into silence, I peeked from under my arms and saw...emptiness.

Above and below us was formless black. Around us was amorphous dark. Only a soft, golden glow remained to relieve the darkness, and it seemed focused entirely on the four of us.

I skimmed a look toward Archie, who stood with a tennis-ball-sized light orb in the center of each upturned palm.

Sebille unfolded herself from her crouch and glared around. "Are we dead?"

Alice skimmed her hands over her vest as if removing dust from its multi-tasking surface. "We must be. Though, I'll admit I thought there'd be much more pain in being eaten."

Archie sighed. "We're in a void bubble. We're perfectly safe here."

My eyes went wide. "You created a void?"

He frowned. "Not created, no. These bubbles exist everywhere. One has only to access them."

Useful.

I straightened and reached into the darkness, looking for a wall. "How big is it?"

"From a physical perspective, it's endless."

"What other perspective is there?" Sebille asked, giving me an uncomfortable glance.

"Why, metaphysical, of course. In metaphysics, true space is merely a thought concept. While zero space is a concrete entity."

"Yeah, uh-huh," I said, faking understanding. "Makes sense."

Sebille stared at me for a long moment, and I

thought I saw her eyelids twitch. I waited, but her iridescent eyebibbles didn't roll. Though, I was pretty sure she was dying to give them a spin.

"How long must we stay here, Pudsy," Alice asked, rubbing her chubby arms as if she were cold.

It wasn't cold in the void. Not really. But compared to the sauna-like heat of the prehistoric Jungle, it did seem coolish.

Archie shrugged. "Until that beastie leaves."

"How will we know when it leaves?" I asked.

He pursed his lips thoughtfully. "Hold on." The sorcerer stuck his head through the black fabric of the void, disappearing from the neck up.

"And that's not creepy at all," Sebille mumbled.

I nodded my agreement.

Archie yanked his head back, the void bending toward him in the shape of a really big head. The distinct ridges of enormous teeth pressed shapes into the blackness. "Perhaps we'll sit here for a bit, yeah?" He said, sounding breathless.

Gone was his clipped, slightly snotty British accent as he took a couple of steps away from the spot where he'd nearly lost his head.

"Okay, then," I said. "Seems like a good time to take stock."

Alice nodded.

Archie threw his hands up, flinging the balls of glowing magic into the blackness high above our

heads. The spheres hovered in the velvety dark, illuminating a slightly larger area around us. He
dropped onto the smooth surface beneath our feet,
his expression weary and his color slightly gray in
the light of the orbs.

"We need a plan," Sebille said, frowning. "We
can't just keep traipsing around that jungle until
something eats us."

I nodded my agreement. "How are we going to
find the kids?" I asked, biting my lip. "This place is
vast and...crowded with green stuff and killing
reptiles. Finding them in this is like trying to find the
head of a pin in a garbage dump."

As I spoke the words aloud for the first time
since arriving, nausea bloomed in my belly, and my
hands started to shake. Fear consumed me as I realized there was very little chance we'd find Mr.
Wicked, Mr. Slimy, and Hobs. Pretty much zero
chance if I was being honest with myself.

Tears slid down my cheeks.

"And then there's the other issue," Alice said,
throwing me an apologetic look. "We need to find a
way to get home."

"We have no way to get home!" Archie bellowed,
his gray complexion gaining a slightly purple hue.
"We have no Tildy and no way to call her back."

"Maybe Rustin will see her squatting in the
middle of the store and figure out what happened," I
offered, not really believing it was possible.

Sebille perked up. "He might! If he sees the turtle and doesn't see us, he'll look for a way to find us."

Archie expelled air. "He won't realize we're missing for days. And if he does, it would be a miracle for him to figure out the exact pattern he needed to press on Tildy's shell to arrive back here."

"There is a Return button on the key," Alice said, her frown softening. "If he presses that, Tildy will return directly where she visited last."

"Is it clearly marked?" Archie barked out.

Alice's shoulders rounded. "No."

"Then the boy won't be able to use it. Only someone who is familiar with the tortoise and her magic would be able to figure out the key."

"It's the only hope we have," Alice said, glaring at Archie. "Being a Negative Neville isn't very helpful."

Archie made a visible effort to calm himself and then inclined his chin. When he spoke again, his tone was carefully modulated. He sounded like his old, snotty self again. "You are correct, Alice. I apologize. I'm open to any suggestions."

I chewed on my lip for a beat as silence filled the void. Finally, I took a deep breath and said what I'd been thinking since we'd taken off through the jungle. "I think we should go back."

"Of course we should go back, Naida!" Sebille snarled. "That's the problem. We can't."

I shook my head. "I don't mean back home. Well...I do want to go back home...but that's not what I meant by *back*. I mean, we should go back to that lake." Goddess help me. I never thought I'd say those words. The place terrified me. But I couldn't shake the feeling that we shouldn't have left that area. "Think about it. Tildy has landed there twice. If Rustin, by some miracle of the Universe, finds his way here, that is presumably where he will land. And the kids..." I swallowed the fear that clogged my throat. "If they're still..." I couldn't say the word. It stuck in my throat like a fist. "If they're trying to get home, they'll stay pretty close too."

Sebille snorted. "You think Hobs is going to be that rational?"

"Maybe not. But Wicked will. And Slimy's very analytical these days."

We sat in thoughtful silence for a moment, our expressions communally grim.

Finally, Archie sighed. "You're right. We'll go back. We'll have a better chance of finding food and water there, anyway."

"We'll find a lot more than food and water there," Alice griped. "Every dinosaur within miles travels to that lake for water. It's a hotbed of enormous, deadly reptiles."

"Yes," Archie said. "But I agree with Naida. I think it's our best chance of finding everything we're looking for."

Ultimately, we all agreed.

Decision made, Archie risked another peek, pushing only his eyes and nose through the void barrier, just in case. He retreated rapidly enough to let me know the danger had not passed.

We settled in, ate protein bars that tasted like sticky sawdust, and sipped from the small stores of water we had with us. Then, exhausted from a bad night of sleep and nearly constant terror and worry, I curled up in a ball on the amorphous, uncomfortable floor of the void and fell asleep.

I have no idea how much time passed. There was no change of light to indicate the passage of days or hours. When I couldn't sleep anymore, I lay there and stared into the darkness, Archie's little balls of energy having winked out sometime after he fell asleep.

I thought of my missing friends, wishing we were all back at Croakies, safe and comfortable and happy. Tears slipped down my face and filtered into the fabric of the void.

After a while I heard movement, and an orb of golden light reappeared about where I'd last seen Archie. He didn't speak. He simply stood, stretched mightily, and stuck his head through the void.

He didn't pop back right away, making me sit up

with excitement. After a moment, he moved his shoulders through, his body twisting as I envisioned him looking around the entire cave. Then he disappeared with a soft pop. His glow balls disappeared with him, leaving us in darkness.

"Ah!" I screamed, lunging for the spot where he'd been.

Sebille's bright hair popped up next to me, so vivid it was visible through the darkness. "Did he just leave us here?"

Alice yawned. "He'll be back. He's just checking out the area."

Sebille whipped around and I envisioned her glaring at the former Keeper. "What if he's killed out there? How are we going to get out of this void?"

"Oh." The single word was spoken softly, reverberating with uncertainty. "You do have a point."

We waited in taut silence, the three of us pressing closer together with every passing moment, until I was wearing Sebille like a jacket and Alice like a fanny pack.

Just when we started to panic in earnest, tiny, multi-hued stars burst on the air around us, dancing to a manic tune we couldn't hear.

The magic tickled against my skin, eating away a tiny bit of the blackness surrounding us with every touch.

Slowly but steadily, the cave where we'd been

started to reemerge. Moments later, the void was gone.

A horrible stench attacked my nostrils. I sniffed, grimacing. "What is that?" When I tried to move, one foot squished. *Uh oh!*

I looked down and realized I was standing in something slimy and cold. Something that smelled like a garbage dump. I grimaced, my left sneaker completely immersed in...

"Dinosaur poop!" Sebille exclaimed, covering her nose and jumping back. "Ugh! Naida, you have to burn that shoe."

I yanked my foot from the mess with some difficulty. The slimy, aromatic brown pile was dense and sticky like glue. My foot came out sans sneaker, bringing the impossible stench out with it. The horrible smell followed me across the room when I tried to outrun it.

Alice and Archie were both looking a little green. The three of them far way away from me, hands over their grimacing faces.

"I have to get it off!" I shouted, eyes wild.

"We'll look for a puddle or something along the way," Archie said, his face stuck in a horrified grimace.

"But my shoe...?" I sent a look filled with trepidation toward the thick, brown gel. I could just see the tip of one shoestring sticking out the top of it. "I can't walk through the jungle with only one shoe!" Okay, I'll admit it. My voice might have gone slightly shrill.

Startle the pterodactyls out of the sky shrill.

Sebille's head was whipping violently back and forth. Her iridescent green gaze burned with a horrified gleam. "You aren't going to dig for it, are you?"

I retched at the thought. "I..." Uoohmph. "I have to..." Uoohmph! I locked my lips to keep from hurling onto my last clean sneaker.

Archie pointed toward the cave opening, beyond which a bright sun shone happily over the land. "I have something I need to do." He ran out the door.

Coward.

I sent Alice a pleading look. "Surely, you have something in a pocket?"

Her eyes popped behind the enormous glasses. She backtracked in silence, shaking her bushy head, and then turned and scurried after Archie like the rat she was.

I gave Sebille my most pathetic look.

She blew a raspberry. "Not a chance."

Pathetic turned to ruthless in a heartbeat. "You don't want me to tell everyone about how you clutched me and screeched like a girl when that T-Rex showed up, do you?" I snarled.

Her fiery red brows lowered like angry caterpillars. "You wouldn't dare."

"Oh, yes ma'am, I would." I clutched myself, pasting on a horrified expression. "Ahhhh, help me,

Naida! Save me from the great big Salamander with huge teeth," I sang in a screechy voice.

The caterpillars wrinkled into angry peaks. "I'll murder you in your sleep."

I shrugged. "Do your worst. My life is clearly over."

She stared hard at me for a minute and then sighed. "Okay. I think I have an idea."

The leaf we'd wrapped around my foot slapped wetly down on the path as I trudged forward, my sneaker-clad foot following silently behind. The leaf-shoe was surprisingly resilient, its dense surface giving me protection from the small rocks and sticks we encountered along the narrow, winding path.

But it wasn't quiet. And, since it was still shedding droplets of rain from the previous night's storm, it wasn't dry either.

At the front of our single-file line, Archie threw up a hand and we jolted to a stop. I perked my ears, listening for the tell-tale sound of a hunting predator. All I heard was a distant crunching sound that made me shiver.

Something was getting eaten.

Bleurgh!

After a moment, Archie started off again and I

fell in behind Alice, Sebille bringing up the rear. The bright, sunny morning had quickly morphed into a painfully hot afternoon. My entire body was coated in a thick layer of sweat, my clothes soaked through with the stuff, and my aroma the stuff of horror movies.

I slapped at another bird-sized vampire bug, my fingers coming away covered in bright-red blood as its component parts smeared into my sweat and stuck there, legs and wings a puzzle of gory parts.

I'd kill everyone in my party and chew on their bones for a hot shower and clean clothes.

I swallowed at the blood-thirsty thought, reining it in before I initiated a Donner-party-like episode, Jurassic style.

The thought made my stomach rumble. I'd had nothing but a sawdust bar and some berries that Alice declared safe since arriving in the jungle. My stomach was so empty, I was pretty sure my organs had started consuming each other in panic.

Then I remembered the ten extra pounds I hauled with me wherever I went and calmed down. I could live off the fat of my land for at least a few days. As long as I had water.

That thought reminded me I was thirsty. At least the jungle offered plenty of water. "I need a drink," I told my friends. They ground to a stop, looking as miserable as I felt. Imagine how they'd feel if they knew I'd been thinking about gnawing on their bones.

No, Naida! Bad, Naida.

I stepped off the path, looking for some of the massive, dark green leaves we'd drunk from earlier in the day. They had bowl-shaped centers that held the rainwater nicely.

I found one with a good amount of liquid in its bowl and grasped its edges, pressing them inward to form a natural funnel, which I positioned above my lips and tipped.

Cool, clean water ran into my mouth. It tasted like heaven. In fact, I was pretty sure I'd never tasted anything so delicious in my life.

When I'd had my fill to drink, I dumped the rest on my head and closed my eyes as it slipped down my back underneath my sweaty tee-shirt.

"Here."

My eyes snapped open at a crinkling sound. A small bag of nuts dangled from slender fingers in front of my face.

My mouth watered and my stomach growled loudly. "Thank you!" I snatched it from Sebille's grip before she could change her mind. Then shame got the best of me and I hesitated. "Are you sure you want to share? We don't have a lot of food and we don't know how long it will need to last." My lips curved downward as the reality of our situation hit me again. With all the other problems, like being without a shoe or, more important deodorant, and dodging predators at every turn, I'd been able to shove thoughts of never seeing Croakies again from my mind for short periods of time.

"You need it," Sebille said, her voice missing its normally superior tone.

"It's not your fault the Loch Ness Monster ate mine."

She shrugged. "It's not your fault either. Besides, we're going to go home soon. I'm sure of it."

She didn't look sure. In fact, she looked pretty darn unsure. But I appreciated her attempt to stay positive, even though an optimistic Sebille was a terrifying thing. It all but assured that we were doomed.

"We should get moving," Alice said, staring up at the impossibly bright sky. "I figure we have a couple of hours before it gets dark. We do not want to be out here when darkness falls."

I couldn't agree more.

We started off again.

An hour later, I was so miserable and tired that my brain didn't immediately wrap around the sound of thunder in the distance, or wonder what it meant.

When it finally registered, my first thought was that a storm was moving in again. But the air didn't feel moist like it had before the last storm, and there wasn't a single cloud in the sky.

Then I noticed that the ground was shaking.

I stopped abruptly, causing Sebille to slam into me from behind and nearly sending us both to the ground.

"What in the goddess's best Sunday hat are you doing, Naida?" she groused, shoving me away as if I'd been the one to slam into her.

"Don't you hear that?" I asked, my eyes feeling like dinner plates in my face.

She went silent, her expression belligerent for a beat and then slowly morphing to one of concern.

Archie and Alice slowed to a stop several yards up the trail. "Come on, you two," Alice called out. "We need to pick up the pace, or we'll..." Her voice sliced off in the middle of that thought. She glanced down at the ground beneath her sensible shoes.

Two worry lines creased Archie's face.

As one, all four of us turned to stare toward the sound. In the distance, the vegetation shimmied, then started to swish sideways as the thundering increased.

"Holy banshee blisters!" I screamed as I finally realized what we were seeing and hearing. "It's a stampede!" I turned on my heel and plunged from the path. "Run!"

Sebille and I dove into the brush to the right. Archie and Alice dove left. We didn't have time to run very far, but there was a massive tree not too far down the path, so we jumped behind that, crouching close to the ground.

A small herd of some kind of lightweight dinosaur with slender forms and small heads shot past us, moving like cheetahs through the dense vegetation. Behind them, a flock of tiny, pale-green flying dinosaurs with two-foot-long wingspans skimmed the tops of the thick, shiny green leaves and shot skyward between the massive, overarching trees, emitting a chorus of throaty squeaks.

"Pterosaurs. Anurognathus!" Archie yelled.

Sebille and I shared a look and she shook her head. "The man's seriously weird."

I couldn't disagree. So I didn't try.

The underbrush a mere ten feet away split, revealing two giantnormous creatures with huge horns and massive bony plates behind their heads. The plated dinos blasted through, leaves swinging from their snouts as they ran.

"Triceratops. Brilliant!" Archie crowed after the thundering creatures passed.

Something else, too small to see beneath the leaves, shot past our feet with a series of high-pitched snorts, leaving a trail of waving plants in its wake.

The thunder of massive footfalls continued, never speeding or slowing.

My heartbeats matched the rhythm of the booming steps and I stopped breathing, only remembering to suck air when my chest began to ache.

Sebille had wrapped her arms around the tree and was doing her best to impersonate bark.

The thunderous footfalls grew closer, never slowing, and I said a silent prayer that whatever it was would just pass us on by. Then a terrifying head came into view, a couple of stories above us, and the horrific sight of a Tyrannosaurus Rex's impossibly huge teeth made my bladder threaten to empty.

"Goddess, goddess, goddess, goddess…" I mumbled in soft prayer. All the blood leeched from my face as the thing lifted its head, its slitted nostrils flaring. I remembered learning about the frightful creatures in school. One thing had forever lodged itself in my brain. The T-Rex was a prime hunting machine. It could smell its prey from miles away, see as well as a hawk, and use echolocation to "hear" its victims from a distance.

Even if we didn't move so much as a toe, that killer reptile would know we were there.

As if it had heard my thoughts, the softball-sized eyes slid toward the tree where we hid. My bones melted. I was a heartbeat away from folding into a terrified puddle of goo on the jungle floor.

I was going to totally embarrass myself in a minute. Forget deodorant. I was going to need a change of undies. Or a diaper.

I sent a silent plea to Archie not to bellow out the genus of the thing waiting mere yards away to eat us. It wasn't like we didn't already know what it was or recognize our imminent deaths on its ugly, horrifying face.

Beside me, Sebille's teeth clacked together as she made like a tree, her eyes closed as if that would keep the monster from seeing her.

I envied her the coping mechanisms. I was too scared to even attempt to hide. I felt my lifelong fatalism take my quivering form over, and with the certainty that I was about to die, I wondered if being eaten would be a quick way to go.

Air soughed in and out of the dinosaur's nostril slits, and something behind its head crawled and writhed.

What in the goddess's favorite spatula was climbing around up there? I squinted. What would ever be that stupid?

"Meow!"

I jumped, gave a terrified screech, and watched Sebille peel herself off the tree like a length of ugly contact paper and run screaming into the jungle with her bony arms waving above her head.

10

YOU'RE KIDDING ME, RIGHT?

My first instinct was to grab up Mr. Wicked and run after Sebille. The Rex would make very short work of my cat and, with Wicked yowling unhappily, as if he blamed me for the fact that he'd ended up in a prehistoric jungle, Rex couldn't possibly miss the fact that we were there.

"Shhhhh!!!!" I urged as panic slipped over me like a spiky blanket.

Thump.

Thump.

Thump.

Sweet goddess in Fred Flintstone's car! It was on the move.

I felt its hot breath mere inches from my face. Clutching Wicked against my chest, I slowly raised my head and grimaced as an enormous blob of T-Rex spit splatted onto my head.

I found myself staring at two rows of massive teeth that were longer than my fingers, and my knees knocked together. *Diaper, diaper, diaper...* I chanted under my breath.

Hot breath snorted against my face, blowing my hair back.

"Yeow!" Wicked complained before slapping the monster on the snout with a tiny, clawed paw.

Godzilla loves a Geisha! All my internal organs seized up in horror. I jerked sideways, putting myself behind the tree, and dug in to start running. I doubted I could outrun the thing. Its stride was forty times mine, but I refused to just stand there until it ate us.

I never took that first step.

Something green and squishy flew through the air and plopped onto a large leaf next to the tree. I looked down into a pair of bulging black eyes. "Slimy?"

What took you so long? the fat squish accused.

Irritation shot up my spine. "You're kidding me, right?"

He blinked. *We thought you guys would never show up. I hate it here. I'm like a short stack with fly syrup around this place. I wouldn't last a minute in that stupid lake. Even the minnows are as big as cars. The last bug I caught with my tongue was so big it reared back and pulled me off the ground. Where's our ride out of here?*

I was pretty sure the frog had just surpassed the record for most metaphors in one burst.

"Meow!" Wicked offered in agreement.

I put a hand on my hip. "Do you two think this has been a party for us? I'm starving, and all we have to eat are sawdust bars. My clothes are so gross that burning is too good for them. I have only one shoe..." I lifted my leaf-clad foot to show them. "And I'm about to become T-Rex kibble." I glared back and forth between them. "At least the stupid King of the Dinosaurs will get dinner. I bet I'll taste better than that tree bark I've been eating."

The bush under Slimy rustled, and he went airborne as a massive snout took a bite out of it. Something flew over the dinosaur's head as he lowered it, sailing past in a dirty blur and disappearing into the jungle in the direction Sebille had gone.

It crashed down in the distance.

I waited for it.

It took a beat.

Then...

"Again!"

My heart soared. I was so happy I almost forgot about the massive reptile chewing a bush and breathing hot air on me.

I frowned at the Rex. "Not that I'm complaining or anything, but why aren't you eating us?"

Slimy sighed. *Trex is a vegetarian*, he said from his spot near my leaf-shoe.

I looked down, certain the frog was pulling my...erm...leaf. "He is not."

Slimy blinked up at me.

The Rex's massive head lifted, throwing shade over us as he rose and rose and rose...

For about the tenth time that day, I dug in and prepared to run for my life.

The Rex opened his blood-chilling maw and ripped a small branch off the tree, chewing happily.

I watched in awe, ducking the bits of wood that fell over me. "Well, I'll be..."

"Naida!" the sprite's voice pierced the moment. "Look what I found!"

"Trex huh?" I asked.

We were all standing on the path, watching the massive reptile eat a tree.

Hobs nodded. "Yes, Miss." He clutched the creature's enormous tail, quivering with excitement as he waited for...

Without warning, the dinosaur whipped his tail sideways and Hobs flew through the air on an extended squeal. He landed in a soft green bush a block away and screamed, "Again!"

"Fascinating," Archie said, staring at the T-Rex. He stood far enough away from the dinosaur to keep from getting stepped on, his arms crossed over his chest and his expression filled with scientific wonder.

"How is it possible that a T-Rex is an herbivore?" Alice asked him.

Archie cupped his chin thoughtfully. "I've never heard of it, but Tyrannosaurus Rex is a Theropod, and several of that genus did evolve to become herbivores and omnivores. It's not entirely unheard of..."

I grinned, watching the terrifying creature pick a branch as big as my leg daintily from its teeth with a claw. Who was he kidding? It was frog-flippin' amazing. Leave it to the troublesome trio to get trapped in the Jurassic era and meet the Universe's only vegetarian T-Rex. "It's brilliant," I said to mimic Archie.

The sorcerer laughed, his eyes twinkling as he glanced my way. "It is, isn't it?"

"Meow," Wicked said, squirming slightly in my arms. His tail whipped beneath my arm as if he was losing patience with being held, but he made no move to try to escape. I suspected I was denting his cool-guy cred, but he was as happy to see me as I was to see him.

He rubbed his soft head along my jaw. I kissed the top of his head.

"Ribbit!"

I glanced at Sebille. Her bony shoulder was green and squishy under a bad case of frog.

Slimy blinked back at me. *Hey*, he said.

I grinned. "Hey, squish. I'm glad you're okay."

He shifted and I got the impression it would have been a shrug if he'd had shoulders. *It was touch and go there for a while. Until we met Trex.*

I eyed the big goof, who was crouching down chewing on a small tree, his butt in the air and tail wagging. I realized that he had to be a young dinosaur. "I can see how he'd be a good guy to have in your corner."

Slimy shifted on Sebille's shoulder, looking antsy.

The sprite narrowed her gaze at him. "Do you need to pee, frog? Because if you pee on my shoulder, you and I are going to have a problem."

I winked at Slimy. "What's the big deal, Sebille? We already smell like a sewer. What's a little frog pee in the grand scheme of things?"

The sprite glowered at me. "I'll tell you what it is. It's the final straw, that's what it is." She swung her arms to indicate the jungle around us. "Do you see a laundromat around here? Because I don't. Whatever lands on the clothes in this jungle stays on the clothes. I don't intend to walk around for the rest of my days with a tiny yellow spot on my shoulder."

"You won't even be able to see it," I teased. "It's a brown shirt."

Her teeth gritted, Sebille ground out, "I'll. Know. It's. There."

I chuckled.

The frog shifted on Sebille's shoulder, his little face pinching. *Um...*

"Arghhhh!" Sebille shrieked. She grabbed the frog and plopped him unceremoniously onto a thick, green leaf. "You just lost your bus privileges, reptile."

"Meow!" Wicked shoved free and dropped down close to Slimy, his tail whipping angrily as he glared at Sebille.

"What?" she shrieked. "He pees on me, and I'm the bad guy?"

A roar vibrated the air around us, rumbling the ground. The sound was soon followed by the thunder of Trex's enormous feet as he hurried toward us, Hobs sitting on his shoulder.

"Fun's over, kids," Alice said. "We need to find shelter. Something scary's coming."

I frowned. "That's just Trex..."

She shook her fluffy head. "I'm talking about whatever the baby dino's afraid of."

"She's right," Archie agreed. "Tyrannosaurus Rex has acute senses. Trex must hear or smell something that worries him. If it worries a forty-foot-long reptile, it should definitely worry us."

We hurried down the path, Trex thundering along behind us. I had to give him credit. For a young creature, he was surprisingly aware of his surroundings and how to place his big feet and tail to keep from splatting us.

Hobs was having a party running up and down Trex's long body, occasionally getting thrown from the tip of Trex's tail and sailing over our heads into the thick vegetation ahead.

He was a constant blur tearing past us back to his gigantic friend, where it all began again.

I started to wonder if the hobgoblin might actually be worn out by the time we reached the lake. Nothing had ever managed to tire him out since I'd known the little guy, but if anything could do it, a trek through the jungle with a house-sized launch pad just might be the thing to get 'er done.

The flow of leathery creatures increased tenfold as our journey grew long. Though they all kept a distance from us, given our giantnormous travel buddy, panic at being caught within Trex's attack zone had nearly gotten us trampled more than once. The closer we came to the lake, the more we had to keep our senses tuned to our surroundings—something that was made more and more difficult by the setting sun and our weariness.

I was stumbling along, picking my way over roots and small, scurrying critters as the last of the light slid toward the tops of the trees. The horizon was painted in a gorgeous spray of pink, purple, and gold. The muted highlights of color were all we had to light our way.

Wicked danced around our feet as if he had all the energy in the world, and Slimy was motionless inside my shirt.

Trex had slowed behind us. Even Hobs was quiet. When I turned and squinted toward them, I could just make out the white of Hobs' favorite outfit through the darkness.

I yawned widely and jumped as a horrifying screech pierced the night.

Ahead of me, Archie's head came up and he went still.

"What is it?" Alice asked him, her voice thick with weariness.

The sound came again, from another direction. Then from behind us. And from directly ahead.

Whatever it was, we were surrounded.

The leaves around us rustled and several dark shapes, looking enormous in the low light, moved closer.

I sucked in a gasp, my bladder quivering at the sight.

What's wrong? The frog asked, his voice filled with trepidation.

"You don't want to know," I murmured softly.

They were big. Not as big as Trex, but big enough to kill us with a single bite. Their bodies were dark, with odd striations of lighter color, like camouflage that would make them nearly impossible to see in the jungle. The crowns of their heads were red, with bony looking ridges over and between the eyes, which glowed yellow in the growing dark.

Creepy, those eyes.

There was a muscular hump in the dinosaurs' necks, just behind the head. They had small arms like the Rex and huge claws, the longest claws in the center of each big foot.

They stared at us, making a low noise that turned my spine to ice.

"Archie?" I breathed as panic swelled through my chest, making it suddenly hard to breathe.

"Allosaurus," he said in a voice barely above a whisper. "Smart, fast, and deadly."

Frog-flogging wonderful!

Wicked pressed against my leg, growling low in his throat and his hair standing on end.

I knew how he felt. "Stay close, buddy," I told him.

A roar pulsed through the night. The four dinosaurs' heads shot up and they answered with their own, less bulky but no less petrifying, snarls.

The darkness high above our heads shifted and Trex pounded toward us, the tiny speck of white no longer sitting on his shoulder.

Thank the goddess for small favors...

A small, white blur shot past me and launched toward the nearest Allosaurus.

"No!" I screamed as Hobs landed on the thing's head and dropped something over its eyes before shooting off in another direction in a blur of motion.

The dinosaur reared back, its tail splintering a medium-sized tree as it thrashed wildly behind it. The monster's head flew up and flailed from side to side, clearly trying to dislodge whatever Hobs had covered its eyes with.

The ground beneath my feet rumbled. I barely realized in time that Trex was nearly on top of me.

Literally.

With a short scream, I plunged off the path and got myself out of the T-Rex's path.

Unfortunately, my movement put me directly into the path of a second Allosaurus. Silent and deadly, the thing lifted its head and stabbed it straight down at me. The enormous maw, filled with teeth as long as my fingers, pounded toward me like a pile-driver.

Panic had me freezing, my mind registering, too late, that it was about to take my head off.

Something slammed into me and I flew sideways, a fire-haired sprite rolling with me as we disappeared beneath a dense, berry-laden bush.

"Meow!"

Sebille sent out a pale green flare of energy and the dinosaur roared in pain, stumbling backward.

Wicked bounded up and past us, disappearing again into the green ocean of brush.

"Come on!" I clutched Sebille's hand and shoved to my feet. We hurried after my cat, keeping low so as not to stick up from the dense tangle of vegetation.

Not too far away, something screamed in pain. Ice painted my spine at the sound. I only hoped Trex was the one causing the pain and not the other way around.

He was our best weapon. If we lost him, we were doomed.

A huge form flew over our heads, landing with a meaty crunch on the ground five feet ahead of us. A massive leg lashed against the ground, enormous claws raking the leaves and spewing cool water and plant guts in our direction.

Without losing a beat, Wicked, Sebille, and I changed direction, careening blindly through the jungle.

Another roar broke the night, drowning out all the others.

We jolted to a stop. My heart beat against my ribs, so hard I was afraid my shirt was pulsing out with each beat like a cartoon character.

The roar sounded again, and something big... really big...unbelievably big...headed our way.

Boom!

The tree next to us swayed.

Boom!

Something took off out of the tree with a sound that was half squawk and half screeching roar.

Boom!

Trickle, trickle, trickle.

Moisture ran down my stomach from the spot where Slimy clung to my bra.

"Oh no you din't!" I yelled.

I didn't mean to, the frog said. *I'm scared*. He actually did sound genuinely sorry for peeing on me. He probably didn't want to be evicted from the bus.

Trex roared into the night. The big thing roared right back.

A loud rustling sound had me whipping around. A massive green leaf smacked me in the face as one of the Allosaurus tore past us, getting the heck out of Dodge.

Boom!

Something that looked like a prehistoric possum shot past, whipping its hairless, muscular tail against my shin.

"Ouch!"

More greenery swished. "Naida? Sebille?"

"Over here, Archie!" I whisper screamed. If the monster heading our way was a T-Rex, I wanted to minimize the chances it would hear us.

Boom!

"Come to us," Archie responded loudly enough for the entire jungle to hear. So much for stealth.

Motioning for Sebille to follow, I snatched

Wicked off the ground and we ran toward the sound of Archie's voice.

Just as we were about to emerge onto the path, a hand snaked out and grabbed my arm.

I gave a little scream.

Sebille shot a bolt of pale green energy into the air, slicing a branch from a tree high over our heads. It cracked in half and dropped to the ground with a resounding crash.

"Oops!" the sprite said.

Archie and Alice were hunkered down behind a large bush that had a woody, pineapple looking trunk.

Boom!

Alice's eyes were enormous.

Hobs shot toward us, skidding to a stop so fast the shock of light brown hair between his big ears fell over his face before drifting back up again. "We need to go, Miss."

Boom!

Trex roared.

"We can't just leave him here alone," I said, my heart breaking.

Hobs shook his head. "We have to, Miss. She's not a plant eater."

"She?" Sebille asked.

Boom!

Another branch broke off the tree across the path and fell mere feet away from the young T Rex.

He roared again.

The thundering tread of the bigger monster sped up as it roared in response.

"It's his mama," Hobs said. "We need to go, Miss!"

I didn't think I'd ever seen Hobs looking so nervous. Given that he was a danger junkie, that was definitely saying something.

A loud, prolonged cracking sound flared into the night. We all jumped as a huge tree fell slowly toward us and crashed to the ground a mere ten yards from where we crouched.

I cranked my head up, and up, and up, and up, and... Well, you get the picture.

"That's got to be the biggest Tyrannosaurus Rex that ever lived," Archie breathed out.

Hobs made a small sound and grabbed my hand. "We got to go!"

And suddenly, the jungle was whipping past me in a green and brown blur.

11

DINO DEBBIE RIDES AGAIN

A mighty roar followed us as we sped away, accompanied by a slightly less mighty roar from Trex. Hobs screeched to a halt near a rock wall and shot away in another blur of dirty white. A beat later, he dumped Sebille at my feet. She was holding my cat, who promptly yowled and swiped at her hand with warning claws, jumping away from her when energy flared around the offended hand.

He trotted over to me, tail high and whipping with temper, and hid valiantly behind my legs.

"Way to hit and run," I told him, grinning.

Sebille glared down at him. "Ungrateful rodent."

Mr. Wicked hissed. His business done, he promptly dropped to his fuzzy butt and began cleaning his front paws.

Another blur ended with Alice wobbling on her

feet next to me, beady eyes crossed. "Blimey! That hobgoblin's faster than frog spit."

Happily ignorant inside my bra, Slimy snickered. *Clearly, she's never seen me spit.*

"I think she meant frog pee," I told him, glowering at my own chest.

Sebille snickered.

The frog was not amused. *I said I was sorry about that.*

A small dust funnel announced the abrupt arrival of Archie. He stumbled forward as Hobs jerked him to a stop, looking slightly green around the gills. "I say. That was a bit unsettling, wasn't it?"

While Archie got his bearings. I looked around, trying to figure out where we were. Despite the growing darkness, the moon was full and the sky was thick with silvery stars. The combined effect was magical and cast a silver light over the jungle. The water-laden surfaces glowed in the illumination, sparking it to life in a way I'd never seen anywhere else.

There was no place so dark as a world where only natural light existed. And, at the same time, no place so bright because there was no man-made illumination competing with it.

The spot where we stood looked familiar, but then every place in the jungle looked pretty much like every other place, so that didn't really mean all that much.

"A cave!" Alice proclaimed with delight, pointing toward a deeper black spot on the face of a charcoal gray rock wall. It rose high above our heads. High enough to make getting to it a challenge. But also high enough that it would be good protection from the things that go chomp in the night.

"How are we going to get up there?" I asked, a bone-deep weariness suddenly making it hard to continue standing.

"I'll do recon...make sure nothing's living in there." Sebille popped into her sprite form and buzzed away, her wings giving off a faint illumination in the moonlight.

I shivered as a moist breeze slashed past, rubbing my arms.

Sebille buzzed back a moment later, hovering in the air at eye-level. "The cavern's not very deep, but there's nothing living in it." She buzzed higher and then dipped, her wings a blur behind her. "There's a narrow pathway up to a flat spot in front of the cave. It's tricky but doable."

I winced, eyeing the distance I'd be falling, because sure as sugar snap peas, I was going to take a wrong step and plunge to my death. "Maybe we could just make a nest down here on the ground."

Alice pshawed me. "Woman-up, Naida. That's a walk in the park."

More like a long plunge off a short ledge.

But then the night exploded into a chorus of

roaring and screaming...much too close for my comfort...and I decided she was right. I mean...how bad could it be?

My knuckles were so white, they glowed in the darkness surrounding the goddess-cursed rock wall I was clinging to like an enormous spider with a door-stopper of a backside. I was spread-eagled against the wall, my face smashed into a surface that was too smooth for hand or footholds over ninety-nine-point-nine-nine-nine percent of the wall. The remaining tiny percentage being the three-inch square area my face was currently smashed against, which, of course, featured a prominent and very sharp projection that was presently piercing my left nostril.

"Come on, Naida, stop being such a derf!" sayeth the goddess-blasphemed sprite who'd easily risen to the cave mouth via a set of pretty, butterfly-shaped wings. The aforementioned wings were currently sparkling happily in direct proportion to my misery.

"I told you," I ground out through clenched teeth. "I'm stuck!"

Unfortunately, the ridiculous wrinkle in the wall that some idiot (a.k.a. the one who didn't need to climb the wall because she could fly past it) had called a ledge had, without warning, shrunk down to a sneeze of rock no wider than my thumb.

Since I was not and never had been a fan of heights, I'd quickly become a fly on the wall and my muscles had locked up on me, making further movement impossible.

Yes, I will admit that everyone else had managed to navigate the sneeze and were currently safely ensconced on the ledge above, blinking down at me. But, in my defense, I'd been carrying the frog in my bra. And, aside from the extra, prodigious weight of the fat squish messing with my balance, the mouthy little cur was always and continually barking at me to stop sweating and twitching because I was causing him to slide down my belly at risk of falling out and going plop on the far, far, distant ground.

"What about me!" I'd exclaimed with the full breadth of my maturity firmly in my grasp. I was pretty sure I had bloody little claw tracks from my bra to my belly-button, where said frog had taken refuge in my waistband.

Thank the goddess for elastic waistbands.

Mmmphh deh momenphg tikkah, sayeth the frog.

Did I mention the elastic waistband?

"I'm working on it!" I snarled toward my waist-line. "I'd like to see you climb this cliff."

Immph doot pbepper ban dube!

"Shut it, amphibian," I responded with all due respect.

Thump!

I went very still. "What was that?" I asked the crowd above me.

"Um…That was nothing, Naida," Archie said in a British-tinted falsetto. "You might want to step up the pace of your ascension, though."

"Good golly Molly in a trolley," I muttered.

Thump!

All the hairs on the back of my neck rose at attention.

Blwhtts blapt?

"Nothing," I told the frog. I pulled air into my lungs and forced my limbs to move, shuffling two inches to the side and trying to mimic a Naida-shaped wall hanging.

Thump! Pfffffttttt…

Warm, moist air painted my back and blew my long, brown hair into my eyes.

"Okay," I said, becoming as rigid as the rock I was impersonating. "Don't lie to me. Am I about to be eaten?"

A strange, choking sound was the only response I got. It sounded strangely like… "Is that laughter? Are you laughing?"

Pfffffttttt.

My poor heart did the chachacha against my ribs. "That's a T-Rex, isn't it? Tell me the truth. I'm about to die, aren't I?"

More laughter. "Really?" I screamed at them.

"I'm about to become dino kibble, and you're all laughing?" If I wasn't afraid that looking up at them would topple me off the wall, I'd give them such a glower! "I hate you all."

Something warm and soft touched the back of my neck. I jumped, yelping. The movement overbalanced me, and my worst nightmare came to life. I started to tip backward on a scream. My hands grappled frantically for a grip, my fingertip slicing on that stupid rock pimple that had previously been jammed up my nose. The fiery shock of pain made me yank my hand away before I thought better of it. That was it. My leaf-wrapped foot slipped off the sneeze. And I suddenly found myself flailing in thin air. My body twisted around as I fell, my arms windmilling, and, for the briefest speck of time, I found myself looking into a pair of enormous dark eyes that appeared as surprised as I felt. Between the eyes, large slitted nostrils flared from a bulging nasal cavity in the small head, which drew back on an impossibly long neck and an enormous body with four tree-trunk-like legs left the ground in alarm. When the dinosaur landed a beat later, the world rumbled and twitched under its prodigious weight.

In pure desperation, I reached for that long neck like a lifeline as I plunged downward. Against my will, my arms wrapped around the thick appendage, clinging for all I was worth.

I hung there, clutching with my arms and legs,

and braced for the creature to spin and run away like a terrified horse.

It didn't. Apparently, my weight wasn't enough to seriously alarm it. A realization that was both comforting and terrifying.

The small head turned in a clear attempt to see the giant bug clinging to its neck. "Whaaaa?" the creature asked in a melodious, almost sweet-sounding voice.

"I'm sorry. I'm sorry. I'm so soooo sorry," I chanted with my eyes squeezed shut. My death was so close I could taste its sour effusion on my tongue.

Mwhattst gongh ongp?

I prayed and clutched, barely breathing.

DNaiptha?

"Not right now, frog," I said, barely above a whisper.

To my shock, the creature I clutched between my legs and arms made a soft warbling sound and began to sway back and forth, a gentle movement that had me cocking one eye open and then the other. The neck I was wrapped around arched beneath me, and the big dark eyes turned my way. Its jaws moved in a leisurely fashion, the partially chewed remains of a fern-like plant dancing at the corner of its lips with the movement.

I watched for a moment, the swaying movement calming my nerves almost as much as the realization that the creature was eating a non-meat item. "Archie?"

"Camarasaurus," he said with an awed tone. "Herbivore. Eats stones to help with digestion, much like our geese of today. That's probably why she's hanging out near this rock wall. Magnificent creature."

I arched a brow at him. "She?"

He nodded toward a spot behind me, where a smaller version of the monster I was hanging off of was nibbling happily on a small evergreen tree.

"Yeesh!" I breathed. "It must be Spring. There are baby monsters everywhere."

Sebille snorted. "These are some big babies."

She wasn't wrong.

Bwillk Shumpbudty ptel bme bwhotts gobin ond?

I sighed. The frog was getting on my last nerve. "We're clinging to a dinosaur's neck about eighteen feet off the ground. Does that make you feel better?"

Croak.

"My sentiments exactly."

"Naida, you'd better do something before she gets spooked and takes off through the jungle," Alice the Helpful offered not so helpfully.

"Ya think?" I snarked back. My mind raced. She wasn't wrong either. I did need to do something. The question was...what?

Warm air bathed my leg, and I looked down into a face that was only a fraction of the size of the mother bear I was riding, but still big enough to scare the leaves off a small tree.

"Warble, warble, waaa?" sayeth the baby Camarasaurus in a sweet voice only slightly tinged by a growl.

"I didn't mean to fall here," I assured the baby. "It was just a terrible, awful, horrible mistake."

"Warble, waaa, wop, werbie?"

"Yeah, sure, kid. Whatever," I said in a sugar-sweet voice. I figured it didn't matter what I said since the baby dino wouldn't understand me any more than I understood it.

The miniature dinosaur turned away, moving slowly toward the rock wall on tree-sized legs. To my shock, the incorrigible kiddo rose up onto its back legs and rested its blocky front legs against the wall. Stretching its neck, which was as long as I was tall, the baby chewed on the rock wall like a teething ring.

Mama watched the baby for a beat, still lazily chewing, and then lumbered toward the wall.

I had to bite back a scream as she moved forward since her long, long neck rocked up and down as she walked.

I was clutching so hard to the thick, slippery appendage that, for a long moment, I didn't realize the dinosaur had moved me a couple of feet from the ledge I'd been trying to reach.

Problem solved.

I looked up into Sebille's grinning face as she offered me a hand. "Come on, Dino Debby," she said. "Time to dismount."

Archie's hand joined Sebille's and, with an answering grin, I forced myself to release the iron grip I had on my reluctant ride and grasp the lifeline they offered me.

12

THINGS TO BE A-VOIDED

I kicked the rock of the cliff wall with my heels, the tattered leaf-shoe Sebille had made me scratching roughly against the smooth, hard surface. Below me, the night was alive with almost constant activity. The moon shined a silver light across the surface of the lake where I'd nearly been eaten, making it look deceptively peaceful, despite the occasional ominous ripple I could see marring its surface.

Beside me, Wicked stretched and yawned, then curled into a ball and sighed. I stroked his soft fur, thankful for his warm weight against my thigh.

Behind me, soft conversation punctuated the rumble of life below, and the comforting scent of woodsmoke filled the air.

A pebble skipped across the ground and plunged over the edge. I looked up to find Archie lowering himself to a seat beside me. "Hey," I said, though we'd been within ten feet of each other for the hours since we'd arrived at the cave.

"Naida Keeper," he said, his teeth gleaming white in a quick smile. "You should try to get some rest."

I shrugged. My mind was far too busy for that to ever happen. "I will soon."

We sat in companionable silence as Sebille and Alice settled down to sleep behind us.

My mind returned to its convoluted thoughts, replete with worries, regrets, and questions about our future. "Are we going to die here?"

I hadn't known I was going to ask the question until it was out there, floating between us like a particularly potent stink bomb.

Archie shifted uncomfortably. I wasn't sure if it was because of my question or the array of little rocks littering the ledge's surface. He didn't respond for a long moment and then sighed. "I hope not." He dropped an arm around my shoulders, giving me a brief squeeze that made tears prickle in my eyes.

A change of topic was required. "Why did you spell me to forget you?" I asked. I turned to see his reaction to my question.

He flinched slightly and then his shoulders rounded. He looked miserable. "It's complicated."

I laughed unhappily. "We have nothing but time."

He looked up at the star-drenched sky and I followed his line of sight. No matter how many times I looked up at the impossibly beautiful sight, it still surprised and delighted me. I wondered if there had actually been more stars in the sky millions of years ago or if they were just harder to see in a modern setting.

Probably a bit of both.

By the time he finally responded, I'd nearly forgotten I'd asked the question.

"I wasn't to make myself known to you."

I frowned. "Why not?"

He shrugged. "A promise to someone who is dear to me."

I half turned, drawing one leg up and wrapping my arms around it. "Who would ask you to make that promise?" All the questions I'd nurtured from the time I was old enough to wonder about my heritage surged forward and waited at the back of my tongue, eager to be answered.

He shook his head, plucking a stone off the ground and flinging it toward the black void below.

"Tell me," I implored. "I deserve to know."

He turned to me, his eyes black, unreadable pools in the darkness. "I can't."

Anger swept me. "You should have just stayed out of my life then."

He sighed again but didn't try to defend himself.

After a moment, he asked, "Why didn't you read the letter I gave you?"

"How do you know I didn't?"

"Because, if you had, you'd be asking me different questions."

My eyes went wide. Ah. He wasn't refusing to give me information. He was only refusing to give me certain information. Okay then.

I thought about the little I'd read of it, the words burnt into my mind despite the energy with which I'd tried to suppress them.

Dear Naida,

I know this letter will come as a surprise to you... perhaps even a shock. But if you've received it now, then it's time for you to know about your past. First, let me tell you that I'm very sorry to have left you on your own for this long. It was a cruelty, yes. But a necessary one.

I've done...things...I'm not proud of. I've brought danger down on my own head, and I'd only hoped to spare you from my poor choices. To do that, I had to remove myself from your life. Of all the things plaguing my existence, that is the thing that takes the largest chunk from my heart. Don't blame Archie. He did the best he could. If he was unequal to the task, that is not his fault. He simply didn't understand. That too was my fault...

What I didn't know because fear had made me shove the letter back inside its accursed envelope and hide it under a bunch of magical texts, was who had written the letter.

But I could guess.

"My mother wrote the letter, didn't she?"

Archie shifted again but didn't respond.

I swallowed the enormous lump clogging my throat, blood rushing to my face and turning it to fire. My pulse throbbed in my head, and it was loud enough to drown out the sounds around me. Fear made it hard to breathe. "Is…" I swallowed again. "Is she alive?"

Archie expelled air in a rush. When I looked at him, he seemed to have deflated. I didn't know if his softer posture indicated relief or abject sadness. Until he opened his mouth and said, "Yes." The single word was spoken so softly I almost didn't hear it.

So many questions. I had no idea where to start. Pulling air into my lungs, I released it slowly, trying to calm the pounding in my head. A moment later, I felt slightly calmer. I rested my cheek on my knee and stared at the distant horizon. It had begun to lighten. I was no Eagle Scout, but I guessed that meant we were a couple of hours from dawn.

When I didn't manage to utter any more questions, Archie said. "Go ahead and ask, Naida."

It was the nudge I needed. "Where is she?"

He shook his head. "I wish I knew. I haven't seen

her since she gave me that letter and asked me to deliver it to you when you'd found your legacy."

I thought about that for a moment, not liking his answer. Unfortunately, I believed him. He didn't know where she was. And it clearly bothered him. "Who are you?"

He blinked as if surprised I'd asked him that. Then he laughed, shaking his head. "I'm your uncle."

I gasped. I hadn't thought I had any living relatives. My gaze skimmed over his shadowed face, seeing only the vague impression of the features I'd recognized despite not understanding that I had. The blue eyes, so like mine. The brown hair, the color of chestnuts and wild with curls. The curls I hadn't inherited, but the color was exactly the same shade as my hair. "Are you her brother?"

He shook his head. Unbelievably, I thought I saw tears glistening in his blue eyes. "No."

He seemed unwilling to say more, so I let silence sit between us for a few beats. If he was my uncle and it wasn't on my mother's side, then...

My throat threatened to close again. "My father," I breathed out.

Archie sniffled, the sound like a bullet to my chest. My father was dead.

I'd always known it in my heart, but learning I hadn't lost both parents as I'd always believed had given me hope...just for a moment...that maybe he was still alive too. "How?" I asked Archie.

He didn't ask me to clarify my question. He sniffed again, dragging his sleeve over his eyes. "We aren't sure."

"But..."

Archie lifted his hand. "I can't tell you more than that, child. Please don't ask any more questions about him."

I fought anger mixed with curiosity. I had a right to know about my parents. Knowing my mother was alive and my father's death was cloaked in mystery, I knew I wouldn't be able to let it go. I'd found myself embroiled in a lot of mysteries lately. I didn't fancy myself good at solving them. I'd mostly just bumbled along until the answer had smacked me between the eyes. But I *had* solved them. And I would solve the mystery of what had happened to my parents. I made myself that promise as I sat in the Jurassic era surrounded by a cacophony of roars, growls, rumbles, and screams.

Somehow, I'd find a way back to Croakies. And when I did, I'd read that banshee blistered letter. No more scaredy Naida. I was going to put on my big girl panties and take charge of my life.

I squared my shoulders and shoved to my feet. "I'm going to try to get some sleep."

He didn't respond.

I left Archie staring out at the trail painted across

the lake by a heavy moon. And felt some small consolation that his secrets were hurting him almost as much as they were me.

If it had been up to me, we'd have stayed in that cave until our ride from the future showed up. But, since there was no guarantee Tildy would ever show back up to fetch us, we really didn't have the luxury of hunkering down.

We needed water. And, if we were going to stay in the jungle...gulp...we'd need to figure out a food source too.

I grimaced at the thought. The last thing I ever wanted to do was kill and eat a dinosaur. It just seemed so wrong. I mean, technically, they should be on the extinct species list. It was against the law to eat nearly extinct species.

Even if they tried to eat me first.

"How are we going to kill them?" I asked. The logistics were overwhelming. Every one of the dinos we'd seen so far had tough skin, not to mention teeth and claws as big as my entire hand. We had no weapons.

Except for a little sprite magic.

Alice's and my magic only worked for calling artifacts. Aside from the magical tortoise I was pretty sure there weren't any artifacts in the Jurassic era.

And, since Tildy hadn't answered my call, she wasn't even there. Archie was a void sorcerer. I probably don't need to explain how limited that was for catching dinner.

Nope, it was the sprite or...

Something flashed into the clearing below us. Something big and wide with...was that a shell? But by the time I focused my surprised gaze on the spot, whatever it had been was gone.

I shook my head, squeezing my eyes shut for a beat and then reopening them.

Nothing.

Dehydration and hunger were clearly messing with me. I was seeing things. I looked at the block of sawdust I was clutching between my fingers and grimaced. If we ever got home, I was never going to eat another protein bar again.

Never.

Well, unless they came in taco flavor. But there had to be actual meat involved in that taco.

I immediately regretted the thought as my mouth watered and my stomach gave off a long, embarrassingly loud grumble.

A canvas canteen appeared in front of my face. I looked up at Sebille, taking the offered water. It felt light. "It's almost gone."

She nodded. "Pickin's are going to be slim for fresh water by now. The plants will have been harvested, or the sun will have evaporated the water on them. I'm hoping for another rainstorm."

I nodded as she dropped down beside me. "I guess we could boil some of the water from the lake." We both looked out at the body of water in question. It was thick with dinosaurs, whose nasty feet and butts were currently moving around in that water. I remembered how cloudy it had been when I'd been fighting to reach the surface before I drowned. That water was more solid than liquid.

"Erg," I said. There was always Alice's straw thing, but I didn't trust one little straw to filter out all that dinosaur butt bacteria.

Sebille sighed. "Maybe it'll rain."

The sky above us was clear and blue, the sun already pounding down on our heads.

Footsteps sounded on the ground behind us, and we turned to find Archie and Alice joining us. Their expressions looked as bleak as ours.

"Archie's come up with a plan," Alice said. She frowned as she said it, her opinion of Archie's plan apparently not good.

Archie threw her a look. "It's not a horrible plan, Alice. I think that maybe...possibly...it could work."

"Way to be forceful, Arch," Sebille teased.

"Why do I have a feeling I'm going to hate this plan?" I asked.

"I won't lie," Alice said, crossing her arms over her chest. "It's a bloody dodgy plan."

"Have you come up with better?" Archie asked, clearly ticked.

Alice pinched her lips together and looked at her feet.

"Yes," Archie said. "That's what I thought."

"What's your plan, Archie?" Sebille asked. Amazingly, she seemed relaxed, as if she hadn't a care in the world.

If ever I needed proof the woman was crazy, that would just about do it.

"Voids."

I blinked at him.

Sebille blinked at him.

Alice gave an exaggerated sigh.

"The absence of anything, hole in existence, nothing and nowhere abysses? Are those the voids you're referring to?" Sebille asked, frowning.

"Well, yes," Archie said. "But there's more to them than that."

A teeny, tiny seed of hope sprouted in my belly. "Can they be used to move us through time and space? Like Tildy?"

"I'm not entirely certain..."

"It seems bloody unlikely," Alice groused out.

"Woman!" Archie barked.

She held up her hands in surrender.

"There was a study written by one Alexander Delicious in eighteen forty-three. Mr. Delicious..."

I rolled my lips together and Sebille snorted.

"Please, Pudsy," Alice said. "Never say those two words together again."

He looked confused for a moment, and then his eyes widened. "Oh. Oh my. Well, be that as it may..." He shook his head. "Alexander posited that voids were not random entities as we'd once presumed. He believed they lay along tracks and pathways, sometimes crossing and sometimes running in parallel trajectories. He even attempted to map the voids..."

I leaned forward, intrigued despite myself. "Have you seen the map?"

Archie's shoulders slumped. "Unfortunately, the pathways of Mr....erm...Alexander's void map ran in suspiciously similar patterns to lei lines. The magical community dismissed his research and presumed he was either a fraud or that he'd mistaken the lei line sink patterns for void activity. While it is true that an interdimensional crossing can sometimes present as a black hole in the Universe..."

I felt my eyes crossing. Archie was about to fall too deep into the weeds and we might never drag him back out. "Archie."

He stopped, glanced my way, and his cheeks flushed. "Yes, well, suffice it to say, his speculations were discredited."

"And that applies to your plan, how?" Sebille asked.

Archie frowned. "I studied Alexander's treatise

on void peculiarities. The man made a very good case. My own studies of the Universal voids would, at least on some level, support his findings."

"Okay..." I said, lifting my brows.

Air exploded from Alice. "You're making a right mash of it, Pudsy. Let me tell them." She looked at Sebille and me. "Archie believes we can void hop through time and space and eventually find our way home."

I thought about that for a moment, the idea so outside my knowledge or experience I wasn't even sure what my feelings about the proposal were.

Sebille's silence told me she was probably trying to wrap her mind around it too.

Finally, I said. "Let's say for a moment that this is possible." Archie opened his mouth, but I held up a hand to stop him. "Hold on," I said. "Let me ask my question."

He nodded. "Very well."

"*If* we are able to hop the voids as Alice said, how long will it take us to get back to Croakies in the correct timeline?"

Archie's lips moved, but no words came out. He closed his mouth, frowned, and then looked at his folded hands. A beat later, his mouth opened again. It hung open without moving for so long that I began to believe he was stuck.

Then, finally, he sighed and said, "I'm not sure."

"Take a wild guess," Sebille said, her tone impatient.

"It could take a few days…"

I frowned. I didn't like the sound of that. But it wasn't horrible when compared to the alternative, which was dinosaur steaks for the rest of our lives. "Okay, that's not too ba…"

"Or, it could take a thousand years."

My lips snapped closed.

Brontosaurus burgers!

That was not good news.

13

WHAT AM I, SAUTEED FROG LEGS?

I peered down at my bloodied knees, hissing as I tugged a small sliver of rock from one of them.

"Woman up," Sebille groused. "It's just a little scuff."

I held the bloody shard up between us. "This is a stabbing, not a scuff."

Her eyes slid upward on the muscle-tracks she'd formed over a lifetime of eye-rolls.

"Don't you roll your eyes at me, sprite!" I groused back. "You didn't have to climb down that stupid cliff face. You got to fly."

Trust me, said the frog who'd ridden in my bra for the trip. *It was no day at the amusement park.*

Sebille shook her head, clearly disgusted with both of us.

"I seem to remember someone clutching me like a girl, knees knocking as she whimpered in fear not too long ago." The words were out before I could stop them.

Sebille went very still, skimming a hostile glare my way. "You promised you wouldn't talk about that."

I shrugged. "I don't want to. I really don't. But certain situations just dig that memory right out of my lockbox and shove it forward."

Hands on bony hips, Sebille glared at me. "Certain situations?"

"You know, eye-rolling, glowering, name-calling. That kind of thing."

Sebille forced a tight smile. "Naida, *dear*, would you like me to heal your knees?"

I ignored the fact that she'd spat the words from her mouth as if they were coated in dinosaur poo. "Why, thank you very much, Sebille. That would be kind of you."

Crouching in front of me, she held her palms over my battered knees and a green glow shot out of them, flaring hotly across my broken flesh. The healing energy burned as it healed, but I bit my tongue rather than let her know how much it hurt.

I could woman up when I needed to.

Yes, I could.

"Come on, you two!" Alice called out from somewhere down by the lake. "We need to get this done before the next group arrives."

Hey! yelled Slimy. *What am I, sauteed frog legs?*

Alice snorted. "You're not driving the bus," she explained to the frog, who apparently suffered from a fear of not being included.

Goddess save me from insecure amphibians.

After careful observation over the last couple of days, we'd determined that dinosaurs arrived at the watering hole in three sort of regular waves. The first wave was just after dawn and consisted of the families, which I found adorable. No matter how fierce the parents, they seemed suitably patient and focused as they bustled their small fry...a relative term in the Jurassic era...to the lake to drink and play, and sometimes fish.

The next wave came about three hours later. That wave seemed to be the herd groups, including an array of adults, heavy on females, with a few children included. We'd observed the final wave the night before. It included single adolescents and elders, both factions eager to pick a fight. I'd ended up quivering at the back of the shallow cave during that wave. There'd been much roaring and slashing and bloodletting before it was all said and done.

Of course there were the occasional loners who showed up whenever the mood hit them. Unfortunately, those included a gnarled and battered T-Rex with one "arm" missing and an enormous dinosaur with huge spikes along its back. That guy seemed to arrive from the water rather than through the jungle, making his arrival harder to detect. He was big enough to chase the gnarled T-Rex away. We'd dubbed him Spiny and unanimously agreed we'd do well to avoid either of them.

The day before, we'd made a group decision to stick close to the cave face, observe and plan for a foray out to get food and water. We'd carefully rationed our remaining water, apportioned what was left of our backpack food, and watched the lake area to get the lay of the land.

We'd come up with a plan.

Wicked, Hobs, and Archie were going into the jungle to search for voids. Archie wanted to map out the local voids in the hopes of compiling a longer-range plan for our dubious void-hopping trip home.

Alice, Sebille, Slimy, and I were in charge of gathering food and water.

Group A, for Archie, had left just after dawn. We hadn't heard from them since.

Group B, for *Because* we couldn't both be Group A and Alice insisted she was running the operation, waited until the dinosaur families finished romping around the lake and ambled away before making our way down the cliff face in search of water and food.

Unfortunately, the family groups had hung around for a good two hours. By the time I'd half climbed and half fallen to the ground, we'd cut our timeline very short.

The herds were due to arrive all too soon.

My healing complete, Sebille turned and stalked toward the lake without another word.

Examining my previously mangled flesh through my torn jeans, I found it smooth and pink. Bending each leg slowly, I determined I was sea-worthy again.

Or, as I gave the glossy surface of the monster-filled lake a wary glance, land-worthy. There was no way I was going into that water again, even with the promise of a plate of tacos.

I frowned.

Well, maybe if there was a donut on the plate too. And an egg roll or two.

Everybody had a price.

My stomach growled. My mouth watered.

Mistake. *Stop thinking about food, Naida!*

The dirt behind me shot into the air and something bumped into my butt. I stumbled forward on a cry and whipped around as a shadow closed on the air. The dirt settled back down to the ground.

There was nothing there.

I peered at the spot, silvery energy spitting off my fingertips. I hadn't even realized I'd called for my power.

When nothing moved or attacked, I did a mental shrug and headed down to the lake. Alice and Sebille were bent over something on the ground.

Something that looked vaguely familiar.

"What's that?" I asked as I approached.

Sebille grasped a muddy swatch of once-red

canvas off the ground and held it up in front of me. The remains of my pack were black with slimy silt and shredded from the massive teeth that had been trying to shred me.

"My pack!" I said, grinning. "Is there anything left?"

Alice held up a flashlight, bent and pierced as if the monster had chewed on it before spitting it out.

I grimaced. "I guess it was too much to hope for."

Sebille made a happy sound of discovery, tugging the zipped plastic bag containing the protein bars she'd given me out of the mess. "The wonders of modern packaging." She danced it in the air. "No water inside."

Thank the goddess. I grinned back.

"Brilliant!" Alice proclaimed. She held up two bottles of water. "These somehow managed not to get pierced."

Sweet Caroline on a unicycle! We had food and water.

We made a small pile with the items and then spread out along the shore, looking for berries and anything else edible. When the distant thunder of dinosaur feet sounded a short time later, we had a pretty good collection of loot.

"We need to get back," Sebille said. "It will take us a while to get Lumbering Linda there up the cliff."

"Har," I said, glaring at her. We gathered up our loot and headed toward the cave.

Alice, whose pockets we'd filled with bars so we could fill the baggie with berries, crinkled when she walked.

I swished and gurgled since I was carrying the water. Sebille held several pieces of some kind of yellow-skinned fruit in her shirt.

We were halfway there when a single *thud* made us halt in shock and fear. The sound was way too close. And the rustling of trees that followed quickly on its heels indicated whatever it was, was no more than ten yards away from us.

We shared a quick glance, my heart thudding hard against my ribs.

Thud!

Rustle, rustle, creak.

Watch out! Slimy screamed in my mind.

An enormous head shot free of the treetops. A bladder-emptying gaze locked onto us. The horrible maw opened wide on a roar, and the thing stepped free of the trees. The massive spikes along its back quivered with rage and excitement.

"It's the spiny one," Alice breathed. "Run!"

The colossal creature surged forward, its enormous mouth opening on a fang-filled roar. The force of its rapidly approaching footfalls shook my entire body, vibrating my teeth until they clacked together. My heart juddered painfully in my chest.

Run faster! screamed the frog.

A small tree cracked and crunched as the

monster plowed right through it, sending it flying. The tree crashed down hard, the violence of its landing sending it skimming along the ground. I screamed, arms flying up as it swept my legs right out from under me. I flew into the air on a terrified scream, knowing that if I fell, the monster thundering my way would kill me before I had a chance to react.

Hot breath oozed over me. Sebille snapped into sprite form and slammed to a stop above me, shooting twin streams of deeply green energy right into the dinosaur's face.

The huge reptile skidded to a stop on an enraged bellow, swiping at its face with its too-small forelegs.

The air beside me sucked inward, dust flew into the air, and something landed hard in the dirt. A silent explosion sucked all the air out of the space. I turned, coughing violently as I tried to shove to my feet.

Sebille buzzed in my direction, screaming something I couldn't hear over the dinosaur's bellows.

The spiny dinosaur was on the move again, heading right for us, and madder than a hippopotamus with a hiatal hernia.

Sebille got right in my face, still screaming. It was all white noise to me. My brain wouldn't register her words. I only had eyes for the creature bearing down on us, one good stomp away from grabbing us up.

Unbelievably, Sebille popped back to normal size, gave me a hard shove that sent me tumbling over onto something hard and round. Having no idea what was happening, I instinctively reached to cover the frog.

Sebille yelled, "Go!"

And somehow, inexplicably, we went.

14

TAKING TILDY AND TASTY TACOS

Spiny wailed and roared and slashed the air, but somehow he wasn't solid enough to touch us. My mind struggled with that, trying to understand why.

The air around us was swirling, filling with pretty pink and green sparkles. A heartbeat later, the ground disappeared from under us, and we were shooting through a familiar, black tunnel. Slimy's tiny heart beat like a piledriver against my fingers.

The long tunnel smelled like home, the scents of books and tea and yesterday's tacos infusing the hollow blackness which stretched out as far as the eye could see. The tunnel narrowed to a point a hundred miles away, a mix of colors melding together at its ending point.

We sailed toward that point, the familiar smells getting stronger as we drew near.

Knowing it would be impossible, I didn't try to see who was driving Tildy. I just embraced the fathomless pit of relief and despair that tightened my gut.

Joy! Sebille, Slimy, and I weren't going to get eaten!

Despair! We'd left our friends behind. Again.

My heart swelled and then burst into a million painful pieces at the thought.

I stared at the endpoint as it rushed toward me, my body vibrating like an unbalanced washing machine. I wanted to land there more than anything in the Universe. But I knew that I wouldn't be able to stay. I had to go back and get Wicked, Hobs, Alice, and Archie.

Tears that couldn't flow bit the insides of my lids. A sob built deep in my chest, my throat tight from its presence there.

The thought of being plunged back into that horrible lake nearly made me pee myself. I was sure I wouldn't survive it a second time.

Without warning, the tunnel flashed away, and the air around us imploded in a silent wash that built agonizing pressure inside my ear.

I doubled over on a groan, my hands clutching the terrified frog. I rolled carefully off Tildy's back and slammed into the carpet at Croakies, cushioning Slimy with my body as I landed.

I rolled to my back, muscles taut as the pressure

eased away. Then, pulling a bracing breath into my lungs, I lifted my head and looked around.

"Meow! Hsssssss!"

I turned to Fenwald, whose tail was snapping angrily from his favorite perch on the sill of Croakies' big window. He was glaring at us as if angry we'd disturbed his sleep.

Ribbit! The squish jumped away and hopped toward the shelves, disappearing into the comforting darkness beneath them. Frantic croaking sounds emerged from the spot where he'd disappeared.

Sebille was lying on her belly next to me, arms spread across the carpet in a wide hug, and making ridiculous kissy noises.

I laughed breathlessly, pushing to a seated position and shoving hair out of my eyes. I looked the place over and found it just as we'd left it. The "Closed" sign was in place, the books were tidy on their shelves, and the paper bag filled with taco wrappings still sat on the nearby table where we'd forgotten it.

The glass of the big picture window looked out onto a dark night, a fat silver moon painting stripes along the carpet.

Sebille sat up too, and she was grinning. "I want tacos! And ice cream!"

I groaned, holding my empty stomach. "Oh my goddess, yes! A big, fat hot fudge brownie boat."

Sebille closed her eyes, groaning happily.

Behind us, someone cleared her throat.

Fenny jumped down from the sill and bounced toward us, his tattered ears going flat against his wide head. "Hsssssss!"

Our heads whipped around.

Sebille's smile slid off her face. In a blink she was standing, with energy spitting at her fingertips.

I made a noise that sounded like a choking guinea pig and jumped to my feet. "Who are you?"

The woman was about my height, around five-nine, with long, straight blonde hair and hazel eyes that glowed with silver energy when she saw Sebille's aggressive reaction. Without warning, her fingers curved and dark gray magic roiled around them.

I held up a hand. "Hold on, let's not start shooting up the place." I glared at Sebille. "We'll listen to what she has to say before we attack."

Fenny sat down in front of me, his wide butt warm and heavy against my leaf-wrapped foot. He watched the woman with a taut awareness that, along with the ridge of lifted hair along his back and the angrily snapping tail, told me he didn't like her at all.

Between us, Tildy chewed placidly on a branch she must have plucked from the tree that had taken me down back at the dinosaur lake. For a massive, lumbering mound of reptile, she could apparently move lightning fast where food was involved.

I could respect that about her.

The thought reminded me...if I was going back for my friends, I needed the tortoise. "Do you have the clicker?" I asked the woman, whose gaze had slid from Sebille to me, warming slightly.

She frowned. "Clicker?" The woman sounded American. No accent that I could discern colored the single word. Her eyes widened suddenly, and she reached into the pocket of her long, frothy skirt. She was dressed like Lea, with a loose-fitting white sweater that hung off one slender shoulder and a wispy oyster, gray, and blue patchwork skirt that flared around her slender ankles. There were gray leather flats on her narrow feet.

The woman held up Tildy's key and smiled. Glancing down at the tortoise, she said, "She has amazing return accuracy."

Thinking about being dumped in the lake the last time, I wasn't so sure about that. "You haven't told us who you are."

"She's a sorceress," Sebille said. She'd let the magic slide away, but she was still glowering at the woman who, probably without meaning to, had saved our lives. "And, unless I miss my guess, she's probably the sorceress Alice has been running from."

A stark silence pulsed between us. When it became obvious the woman wasn't going to respond, I asked, "Is that true?"

Hazel eyes locked on mine. They were kind eyes, surrounded by a thick arc of dark blonde lashes. She pursed well-shaped lips and frowned. "It's complicated."

"Then you'd better get started with the explanation," Sebille growled out. "We have stuff to do."

I threw my assistant a nervous glance. I didn't know what "stuff" she had in mind, but after I grabbed some food and packed another bag, I fully intended to hop a turtle back to the jungle.

The thought twisted my insides into a coil of dread.

The hazel gaze widened. She cocked her head. "You're going back."

I blinked. Was she reading my thoughts? "Tell us who you are."

She frowned. "It's horribly dangerous there."

"Der de der der," Sebille said. "What was your first clue? Oh, right, it was probably the ten-ton monster trying to eat us when you popped in."

"Just stop it!" The sorceress exchanged glares with Sebille. "I'm trying to help."

Sebille snorted her opinion of that statement.

I raised my hands, palms out. "Look, let's all just calm down. Sebille is right. We have a lot to do to get ready."

"To return?"

Why did her question have an angry edge to it?

What was it to her if we threw ourselves back into the land of the dinosaurs? "Yes."

"Why on the goddess's ugly green carpet would you go back to that place?"

Sebille opened her mouth, but I stopped her with a raised hand. "I'll give you four reasons. Our friends who are still stranded there. We need to save them."

She stared at me for a long moment and then, to my shock, nodded. "I understand you are loyal..."

"This isn't about loyalty," I interrupted. But then I realized that was definitely part of it. "Well, it is, yes, but it's also love. Leaving them there wouldn't just make me feel bad. It would break me. Knowing I could save them and not doing it would be the height of selfishness and evil."

She looked like she would speak again, but I shook my head. "No. I don't care what you think. I don't know you, and I don't owe you anything..." I blinked. "Okay, I do owe you a thank you for saving us..."

"No," Sebille said. "We don't even know why she was there. She didn't come to save us. She just dropped into a situation she couldn't control."

"That might be true, but," I started to argue.

The woman sighed. "She's right. Partially at least. I didn't set out to save you. But when I saw the danger you were in, I couldn't refuse help." She shuddered, wrapping her arms around herself. "What a horrid place."

"Why did you go there, then?"

"I didn't. Or, to be clearer, I hadn't meant to." She looked at Tildy's clicker. "I'm afraid I must have pushed *Recall*." She grimaced. "It's right next to the *Refresh* button."

"You were trying to steal the turtle," Sebille said, her tone filled with outrage.

The woman's gaze slid to hers. "Yes."

"Why?" I asked, fear threading through me as I realized she still had control of Tildy. If she decided she wanted to escape with our time traveling reptile...

"Let's just say someone I love needs my help."

We waited another beat, but she didn't offer any more explanation.

"Alice seemed to think you wanted to harm Tildy."

The woman stared at the still munching modern-day dinosaur. Her glance was speculative. It made me very uncomfortable. "Yes, their shells are very powerful."

Sebille and I shared a look. Energy exploded from our fingertips, sizzling through the silence.

The woman shook her head, sighing. "I don't want to harm the tortoise."

She didn't *want* to. But she hadn't said she *wouldn't* harm her. "Please hand the clicker over."

"I don't think so."

Sebille lowered her hands, fingers spread and pointing toward the ground. A thin stream of pale green energy coiled on the air in front of each finger, slipping away and dissipating on the air before going too far.

I felt my eyes widen as an iridescent green illumination flared along the edge of Tildy's shell, sliding around to disappear on the other side.

I didn't know what Sebille had done, but I hoped it was a spell to keep the woman from absconding with our ride.

The sorceress on the other side of the tortoise started to glance down.

I took a step and spoke quickly to distract her. "You can't keep us from saving our friends."

The woman looked amused. "Oh, I assure you, child. I could."

I took another step toward her, praying she kept her gaze on me. "But you won't."

She laughed, the sound light and carefree. "Won't I? Please explain why you believe that. As you took such great care to explain, you don't know me."

"I don't know you. But..." It was my turn to frown. I could feel the woman's magic. It was vibrant and clean, with a thin strand of darkness that felt more sad than evil. I had no idea why I could sense the type of energy she carried. Maybe because she was a fellow sorceress. Though I'd never before been able to *feel* another sorceress's magic. "I believe you'll help us."

The statement hung like a bad smell between us. Or...no...maybe that was Tildy. I eyed the carpet behind the massive turtle.

Yep. A massive, stinky pile of turtle poop steamed beneath her tail. "Awe, really?"

Sebille grimaced and covered her nose. "I'm not cleaning that up."

The woman across the turtle smiled, her eyes sparkling with humor. At that moment, I knew she wasn't evil. At least...not entirely.

To my delight, she shot a burst of gray energy at the pile, and it disappeared in a flash of light.

"Handy," Sebille murmured.

I was relieved. Not only because the air smelled tons better, but because I'd thought I was going to have to use the special hand vacuum we'd gotten during our visit to an interdimensional spot called Plex. The hand vac would make short work of the poop. It could get rid of nearly anything. But the price would have been a bookstore full of songbirds.

We'd been living with about a hundred of the noisy pooping machines for weeks. I'd just managed to coax the last of them outside. I wasn't eager to put more into the atmosphere.

Tildy raised her head and peered at me through eyes that looked like mini-voids. She seemed to be asking for more food.

Apparently, she'd made room in the inn.

"No more eating for you, Missy," Sebille scolded. "What goes in must come out. And I'm not anxious to experience that last little deposit again any time soon."

"I believe she's thirsty," the woman said, her eyes still sparkling with humor.

"That, I can do," Sebille said. She headed toward the tea counter for a dish.

I was left staring at our unwelcome visitor slash savior. "We need to get back to save our friends."

She shook her head. Quick rage flooded my system until she held up a hand. "Simmer down, child. I'm not denying that you should retrieve them. I just wanted to tell you that you have time to rest and restore yourselves."

I was shaking my head before she finished. "You saw what we were dealing with. Alice could be dead already. I can't leave them there, fending off monsters while I rest and eat."

"I don't think you understand how the time travel thing works," she argued. "We can leave tomorrow and arrive whenever you want."

I thought about what she was saying, the concept too confusing for my weary, underfed brain.

"Can we arrive before Spiny strikes?" Sebille asked as she settled a large, low-sided pan filled with water in front of the tortoise.

Tildy stretched out her neck and pressed her

nose into the water, plunging it all the way to the bottom.

"Yes," said the sorceress. "So, as you can see, you have time to rest and recover before we plunge back into that jungle." Her beautiful face softened when she smiled.

I eyed her, wondering what it was about her that had my nerves fizzling like seltzer water. "How do we know you won't take off with Tildy again?"

She frowned. "Tildy?"

I nodded toward the creature who seemed to have parked her nose permanently in the water dish.

"Oh. Yes." She smiled. "I'd forgotten Milly was gone."

"Who's Milly?" Sebille asked, her cell phone clutched in one hand.

"There were originally two of the tortoises. Sisters. I spent most of my time with Tildy's sister. I guess in my mind I was still dealing with her. Sweet creatures." She frowned. "I've missed working with them."

"Were you a turtle handler like Alice?" I asked, suspicion cooling my tone of voice.

"Something like that." She nodded briskly. "Yes, well. I'll leave you to it, then."

My hand shot out and found her slender arm before I'd made a conscious decision to do it. "Where are you going?"

"I'll find someplace. A hotel, perhaps."

For some odd reason, I didn't want to let her leave. I had a suspicion that if she got out of our sight, she'd use that clicker to snatch Tildy from us. "Why don't you..." I glanced at Sebille, but the sprite was already talking to our favorite taco restaurant.

My mouth watered at the thought.

"Stay here," I said before I could change my mind.

The woman blinked. "Er..."

"I mean, I'm going to want to leave in a couple of hours. Despite what you said about having time, I can't shake the feeling that my friends are in terrible danger while I sit here." I didn't add "eating tacos," though I hoped that would be the case. I was pretty sure my internal organs had started chewing on each other. "You can sleep on my couch."

The woman's expression was unreadable. Something silvered her gaze. It almost looked like tears.

I did a mental head shake. It couldn't be tears. That was ridiculous. Alice didn't trust her. I couldn't afford to either. She was probably just trying to make me drop my guard.

"All right. That's very kind of you."

"Nope. Not kind," I told her, frowning. "As long as you control the turtle, I don't want to let you out of my sight."

She tensed briefly and then nodded. "I appreciate the honesty. However brutal." Humor flared in her gaze. "If you'll show me where that couch is, I'll just get out of your way."

Sebille headed for the door. "Be back in five."

Fortunately for us, our favorite taco restaurant was only a mile away, on Arcane Avenue. The same street where Croakies was located.

As the door slammed shut behind the sprite, I said, "You might as well wait and have some food. If I know Sebille, she ordered plenty."

"Oh. All right then. Thank you."

I shrugged, feeling suddenly embarrassed. What in the name of the goddess's worst hairstyle decision had I been thinking?

Oh well, there had to be something to the old adage of "keep your friends close and your enemies closer."

I just needed to figure out which one of those things the woman standing relaxed and unconcerned before me was.

15

THEY'VE A MIND TO HEAVE YER HO

I sat cross-legged in the soft, magical lighting of the artifact library. My eyes were closed, and my hands were resting on my knees, palms upward. Magic danced in my palms, tickling my skin. It was hungry energy, too long away from the thousands of artifacts arrayed in the enormous space.

I pulled air into my lungs, the comforting scent of my own magic and the energy of all those artifacts finally loosening my shoulders and untying the knot in my chest.

Home.

It was a wonderful feeling. There wasn't a flying dinosaur or bad-tempered spiny monster in sight. I sighed, letting my magic slide away from me to paint the air, a reassuring wash of familiar power that eased the slight tension I could feel throbbing through the items within the library.

Something tickled my cheek and I opened my eyes to find the hat feather that had welcomed me on my very first day as Keeper of the Artifacts.

Or rather, as a KOA in training.

Unfortunately, it hadn't been long before Alice had scampered into the next phase of her life and left me to deal with the detritus of her careless keeperdom.

I smiled at the happy feather, which danced on the air in front of me. "Hello. I haven't seen you in a while."

The feather flew away like a shot, dancing between the massive shelving that rose more than thirty feet into the air and stood like steel-spined soldiers throughout the space. Every shelf was full of carefully magicked items that Keepers throughout time had gathered at the whim of the Magical Universe and placed carefully, with magical holds, where they could be watched and kept from harm.

Or, as in the case of the items within the toxic magic vault, kept from harming others.

The room had been utterly still and silent when I'd come into it. But as I loosed my keeper energy through the space, it came alive.

Energy danced around me, lifting the hairs on my arms and vibrating against my skin.

Light speared toward the ceiling high above my head, piercing the shadows with shards of pink and purple, pale silver, and green.

Music burst on the air and the hat that had once held the dancing feather lifted off its shelf and boogied toward me, dipping and twirling through the air with the happy feather as its partner.

The two artifacts danced closer as the music rose and swelled, but I shook my head, sending a slender stream of my energy to ease them back into place. "I've been on the receiving end of your magic before, you two. I'm not doing *that* again." I smiled at the memory.

A squawk high above my head sent a musty red feather drifting down to land on my leg. The sound of clumsily flapping wings filled the sudden silence. SB, the magically bleeped pirate's parrot, fell toward me in a tangle of thrashing wings and grasping claws.

He landed clumsily on the hard floor and skidded in my direction, random feathers dusting the air around him. "Ahoy, Lass! Have ye seen fair seas or foul?"

I grimaced as he tottered closer, his head bobbing energetically with the movement.

"Mostly foul," I admitted. "But I'm going to find a way to make them fairer."

The air sighed, and my hand shot up just in time for Blackbeard's sword to meet my palm. The hilt of the sword warmed and reformed to perfectly fit my grip. I grinned, sliding it through the air in a perfect slicing motion. "No boogies to battle, I'm afraid." I frowned at the thought. "Not any that will succumb to you, at least."

The parrot seemed to think on my response, his ragged form shivering as if trying to coax his feathers into place. "It's a bleepin' long way ye've come. And a bleepin' long way you'll go. Beware what the seas can spawn, for they've a mind to heave yer ho."

I laughed softly. "I'll keep that in mind, SB. Thanks."

I threw the sword into the air and goosed it back toward its high shelf with a wisp of my magic. SB followed it up and settled with a caw before dropping his head and returning to sleep.

"You're very good at your job."

I jumped with a yelp and turned toward the stairs leading to my apartment.

The sorceress sat on a step near the top, her arms hugging her knees and her head lying across them. She was smiling.

I shrugged, feeling self-conscious. "I don't know about that, but it seems to be my calling."

"Indeed it is," she agreed, lifting her head off her knees to nod. "It's your legacy magic."

I frowned. "How do you know?"

"It's as plain as the nose on your face." She straightened. "Let me guess. You first became aware of your power as a young girl." She cocked her head, the silky strands of her light hair falling over her shoulder. "Things followed you around, didn't they? Magical things."

My frowned deepened. "Who are you? How do you know that?"

Her laughter was light, girlish. "It was just a guess. I've..." Her expression grew sad. "I knew a Keeper once. It was how the power came to him."

I thought about that, her words strangely soothing. It was good to know I wasn't some kind of freak. Maybe all Keepers came into their magic the same way. "Well, hopefully, he had more guidance with his magic than I had." I frowned as the words emerged. I hadn't meant to say them. But they were out, floating between us, and I suddenly wanted to walk away from them.

The woman on the stairs was silent.

I shrugged, wishing I could slough the complaint away with the motion.

"I'm sorry," she said softly. So softly, I wasn't sure I'd heard her correctly.

"What?"

The woman gave me a smile that seemed forced. "I said I'm sorry someone let you down. It was an unkind thing to do."

My gaze narrowed on her. Despite the fact I'd sent the complaint into the verbal universe, I felt a sudden need to justify my abandonment. "It wasn't their fault. They died."

She didn't react, only staring at me. Finally, she nodded. "Well, it's still unfortunate."

I couldn't, or, more importantly, wouldn't argue that with her. "You haven't told me your name."

She blinked in surprise. Then laughed softly, shaking her head. "I haven't, have I. I do apologize. I'm afraid the traveling has discombobulated me a bit." She lifted her hand toward me as if offering a handshake. "I'm Narina, Wind Sorceress, at your service."

Grinning, I held my hand out and waved it up and down as if I were shaking her hand, though thirty horizontal and ten vertical feet separated us. "Naida, Keeper of the Artifacts."

"It's a pleasure to meet you, Naida Keeper." Her smile seemed genuine, and her tone was warm.

I dropped my hand and forced my own lips toward neutral, not wanting to give in to her charm. "Why do you want Tildy?"

She seemed surprised at my quick change of subject. "I..." She closed her mouth, swallowed. "I'm searching for someone who's very important to me. I made a promise to him, and I intend to keep it." Her gaze darkened with emotion. "I hoped to use the tortoise to save him."

That didn't sound so terrible. "Why does Alice believe you mean Tildy harm?"

Narina expelled air in a frustrated breath. "I have no idea how that woman gets things into her head.

She has always hated me. I guess that dislike has transformed itself into distrust in her mind."

Her excuse didn't ring true. "Alice can be opinionated and..." I searched for a descriptor that wasn't totally insulting, struggling to find one. The truth was that Alice and I got along like fire and water. "...stubborn..."

"The woman is singularly incapable of completing anything," Narina spat angrily. "She's scatterbrained, unorganized, and has no loyalty whatsoever."

I tensed. While I couldn't argue with the first two, the fact that she was currently running from a nasty dinosaur in the Jurassic jungle firmly disputed the last. "She went millions of years back in time to help me save my friends," I said, my tone more strident than I'd planned. "She didn't have to do that. She did it for me."

"It's the least she could do, after the way she abandoned you," Narina said softly.

I blinked in surprise. *How did she know that?*

I opened my mouth to ask her that exact thing, but she must have realized how her statement would sound. "Yes, I'm well aware of Alice's antics. She and I have been adversaries for a long, long time. I keep tabs on her."

"Then you know about my..." even I had trouble calling what Alice had done training.

"Yes," she said, firmly. "I know she didn't

complete your training. If I'd been in a position to step in, I would have. What she did to you was criminal."

I frowned at the passion in her tone. "Why would you care?"

"I care because I've long been an advocate of better training for new magic users. I used to teach, in fact." She finally smiled, the lines between her eyes softening as she let some of her anger slide away. "Alice would have been drummed out of the Académie d' Magicke for her *teaching* methods."

She said the word "teaching" as if trying to spit a hair off her tongue.

Okay. The strange feeling of having been spied on slid away as I realized Narina had been watching Alice. Not me. "Whatever your feelings about her. She's helping me, and I'll be forever grateful for that," I said, my tone filled with finality.

Narina stood. "I'll turn in now." She climbed the stairs to the landing, stopping with a hand on the banister to look down at me. "I'll be ready to leave at five in the morning." She hesitated as if considering her next words. Finally, she said, "It might be best if just you and I returned." She held my gaze for a long moment and then nodded as if she believed I'd captured her meaning. "Goodnight, Naida Keeper."

I stared after her, wondering why she didn't want Sebille to return with us. Then it hit me, and my stomach twisted with fear. She was afraid we wouldn't make it back.

If I was lost to the jungle, at least Sebille could hold things down at Croakies until I was replaced.

It was a sobering thought. But even worse, I realized it was a sound one.

"Meow!" Fenny wound around my legs, purring loudly. He looked up as I reached to pet him, giving me soft eyes as I scratched behind his tatty ears. "What do you know about her, Fenny?"

His tail snapped the air.

"You don't like her, do you?"

"Hssssss," he said, without much heat.

I sighed. "Yeah, I'm not sure I like her either."

I went to the store to check on Oliver and Slimy before closing up for the night. The two of them were huddled together on Slimy's rock under the heating lamp. I'd given them the last of the crickets while we were waiting for our tacos and some fresh water. "Night boys," I whispered as I reached for the fleece blanket that was draped over the table and pulled it over the top of the aquarium.

Night, said Slimy, a yawn in his voice. *It's good to be home.*

Yes, I thought. It *was* good to be home. I only wished all of my friends were home with us. With that thought dragging me down, I checked the locks on the front door, engaging the magical ward that supported the mechanical locks, then I flipped off the lights and headed through the darkened store to the artifact library. I closed and locked the dividing door by habit, setting an additional ward on it. And then climbed wearily toward my apartment. I hoped the sorceress was asleep, so I wouldn't have to talk to her. I had one more task to accomplish before I could sleep, and it would take careful thought.

Sebille was definitely not going to like the note I planned to leave her.

16

CHA CHA CHA

The return trip to the jungle was much of the same, with my stomach like a fist under my skin and my heart beating the cha cha cha against my ribs.

Narina assured me that she had a handle on our landing and that she'd timed our arrival for ten minutes before the spiny dinosaur emerged from the trees.

Like before, the rich scent of greenery and moist earth assailed my senses as we flew toward the end of the time tunnel. When the heat and light of the open area beside the lake flared suddenly around us, I was more than a little surprised. After the horrible water landing of the last time, I'd been expecting a hard landing at the very least. And a fight to the death in the murky water at worst.

Tildy dropped lightly onto the well-churned ground.

I shook myself out of my stupor, my gaze going to the dust kicking up around the magical tortoise's big feet. A memory slid through my mind. I turned to the sorceress. "Before you landed here the last time, I thought I saw images of Tildy and then felt her shell ram into me, but she didn't land. I told myself I was imagining things."

Narina frowned. "Really? I did do a couple of quick virtual runs, but I hadn't thought I'd gotten that close."

I narrowed my gaze on her. "Virtual runs?"

"Yes," she nodded, flushing with embarrassment. "I hadn't used a magical tortoise for decades. I didn't want to end up somewhere unpalatable."

I had to laugh. "You mean, like the middle of a Jurassic jungle?"

She grinned.

"Naida? Sebille?" Alice's voice called from somewhere along the shore. I pictured the area where Sebille and I had crouched to examine my backpack. A sudden thought brought my eyes wide. "Narina?"

"Hmm?" she was staring at the arch of an enormous fin rising out of the water a hundred feet from shore. The sight made me shudder violently at the memory of nearly being eaten alive as I drowned. "Um…" I shuddered again. "There won't be two of me, will there?" I didn't know why I hadn't thought of that before.

She shook her head, pulling a cell phone from her bag and snapping some pictures of the sea monster. "There will be a hole in the timeline but no duplications."

"What does that mean, exactly?"

She sighed. "It means that whoever you were with will suddenly realize you aren't there. Likely she'll think you just walked away without her realizing it. But you won't have an existing physical presence here because Tildy took you away." She frowned thoughtfully. "It is possible there will be a tiny fold in the timeline, though."

"Meaning?" I asked.

"The sequence of two or more events might be overlaid upon each other."

When my face stayed blank with confusion, she clarified. "If something happened directly behind the timeframe when you disappeared, it could be sped up, overlapping your timeframe slightly."

I thought about that until my head started to hurt.

"Okay, then. Where are the rest of your party?" Narina asked. "We don't have much time."

Alice came around the trees closest to the lake, the tattered remains of my backpack clutched in her hands. "Oh, there you are," she said. "Where did you go? One minute you were with me and then..."

Alice's voice faded away as she spotted Narina. Her eyes went wide. She glanced at Tildy, then at me, and back to the sorceress. "You!" She dropped everything she held and started running in our direction.

Narina watched her come, looking irritated. "You needn't give yourself a heart attack, Alice. I'm not going to steal the tortoise."

Alice stumbled to a walk, her chest heaving from the unaccustomed exercise. She lifted a hand, pointing a rigid digit at Narina. "You just step away from that artifact. You know you have no right to use her."

Narina sighed. "You've certainly told me enough times. Don't get your knickers in a twist. I simply came..."

The trees along the path leading to the caves rustled, and we all turned in surprise as a dingy white blur shot out of them, followed by a low gray form shooting along behind it. Hobs spun to a stop a few feet away, dust spiraling up around his feet. His blue eyes were wide with panic.

It didn't take long to figure out why.

A horrendous screeching filled the air, followed by a panicked shriek of the human variety.

"Archie!" Alice breathed, her beady eyes popping wide behind her smudged glasses.

The man in question shot from the trees and jolted to a stop when he spotted us, his gaze flying to

Tildy, who was unsurprisingly chewing a branch with jagged-edged leaves and tiny red berries.

He threw up his arms. "Oh, thank the goddess!" Running toward us, he screamed. "Let's get this thing out of here!" His hair stood up as if he'd been tugging at it, and the shoulders of his shirt were torn, the flesh beneath it ragged and bloody.

"What happened...?" I started to ask as the first enormous shape shot free of the trees overhead. The pterosaur's wings blocked out the sun as its huge beak opened in another scream.

"It's calling the others," Archie yelled. Bending to pick up a rock, he flung it at the giant flying dinosaur. The pterosaur's wings pounded the air as it tried to avoid the rock, its deadly beak lifting in rage as the projectile slammed into its wide, feathery chest. The flying monster dropped more quickly than I would have thought possible, and its talons raked the air where Archie had been.

He ducked and shot sideways, picking up another rock just as the sky darkened under a new wave of the terrifying creatures.

At that moment, I really wished Sebille was with us. We could have used her magical energy to beat back the one, two, oh my goddess, five enormous dinosaurs swooping toward us with deadly claws and ripping beaks.

I sent a wave of my energy toward them and only succeeded in causing Tildy to shoot in my direction.

Oops! Artifact.

The sharp edge of her shell hit me in my thighs, and I slammed to the ground just as a pterosaur screeched by overhead. Its claws raked the air where my head had been. A sleek, gray form leaped onto Tildy, followed by a white blur.

Panic filled my chest. "Wicked! Hobs! Don't...!"

I grabbed for them, not wanting them to accidentally leave with Tildy and abandon us to the lethal beaks and claws of the enormous flying dinosaurs.

"We need to go, Miss!" Hobs screamed.

"Yes," I agreed. "But not until we get everyone..."

The ground rumbled and a bellow mingled with the screams of the flying monsters.

Goddess on a gilded glider! I thought in frustration. *What now?*

Twisting my head around, I spotted Spiny snatching a pterosaur out of the air, its screeching adding to the general pandemonium that was turning me into a quivering pool of jelly.

I climbed onto Tildy, managing to grab Hobs and Wicked and yank them toward me just as Spiny flung the remains of the unfortunate pterosaur away, its tattered body whipping past mere inches above our heads.

"Get down!" Narina screamed. It took me a beat to realize who it was.

Alice threw herself over Tildy and Archie was

knocked to the ground as another one of Spiny's victims bumped him on its way by.

Apparently, Spiny was having a pterosaur pinata party.

Looking like something the T-Rex dragged in, Archie crawled toward Tildy.

A horrendous *whoosh*! blew through the clearing, the blast so explosive it gusted two of the remaining pterosaurs backward, slamming them into the rock wall housing our little Hades away from home. The creatures hung there, pinned by the force of the wind, as Spiny tried to push his terrifying bulk through the squall to get to us.

He managed one thundering step...and then another...and I realized he was going to force his way through.

I raised my head just enough to see Narina standing with her arms stretched out in front of her, palms out, and silvery magic bathing her to her shoulders as she pushed a dense wall of wind at the determined beast.

Glancing toward Archie, I yelled, "Hurry!" The wind grabbed my words and ripped them away, leaving me wondering if he'd even heard.

Head down against the residual drafts, Archie crawled slowly forward. I clutched Hobs and Wicked in one arm and shoved with my toes, trying to get more of my body onto the tortoise.

On the other side of Tildy, Alice had managed to get her chest and one leg draped over the turtle.

Archie army-crawled toward us, his hair blown straight back from his face and his eyes mere slits against the swirling dust.

A horrific screech tore the air above Archie. To my disbelieving gaze, a pterosaur whose wings had to be thirty feet across dove through the cloud of dust above our heads. It swooped low, its claws clutching poor Archie's already torn shoulders, and ripped him off the ground.

"Archie!" I screamed, half rising to try to get to him. But someone else moved before I could.

No! I screamed inside my head as Hobs shot out of my grip and leaped onto the massive winged dinosaur.

The monster dropped Archie in surprise as Hobs landed on its back. As the creature reared upward in reaction, the little guy lifted skinny arms over his head and smashed something against the pterosaur's pointy head.

With an enraged screech that brought all the little hairs to attention on my body, the pterosaur banked sideways, its form wobbling uncontrollably on the air, and slammed into a huge tree hard enough to break its hollow bones.

Hobs dropped to the ground and disappeared into the whirling dust.

"Hobs!" I shoved upright and was blown sideways immediately, my hair plastered to my face so I couldn't see. I sucked in a mouthful of dust and succumbed to violent coughing.

Spiny gave a final roar and turned toward the water.

Her magical wind cutting off, Narina dropped to her knees as he thundered away, no longer interested in what should have been easy prey. Fortunately, thanks to the sorceress, we'd proven to be much less than easy.

I climbed to my feet and hurried to Narina. "Are you okay?"

She was pale, her hands shaking with weariness, but she nodded. "We need to go."

I couldn't agree more.

Movement out of the corner of my eye had me turning my head in time to find the giant pterosaur plucking itself off the tree. Unbelievably, the monster lifted its wings to fly.

Hobs leaped from the ground, grasping the thing's tail before it could take off.

I shoved to my feet and started to run.

Hobs swung to the flying dinosaur's back just as it gathered wind beneath its wings and shot into the air.

"Hobs, no!" I screamed. Then I skidded to a stop as the little hobgoblin disappeared skyward on the back of the monster.

I turned to the sorceress. "Narina?"

She climbed wearily to her feet, her arms looking like they weighed a hundred pounds as she slowly lifted them. She waited for the right moment as the pterosaur turned and headed back our way. Apparently, the thing was more persistent than Spiny, and it wasn't done trying to get its dinner in that clearing.

To my horror, Hobs' tiny head rose above the pterosaur's pointy crown, and he stood, arms out to the sides as the bird deftly rode the currents.

Even from where I stood, I could see Hobs' grin. He was having fun.

"That stupid creature," Alice breathed beside me.

The little hobgoblin walked up the monster's body to its head. Barely able to breathe, my arms lifted in an unconscious desire to catch Hobs if he fell.

But he wasn't thinking about falling. Not at that moment. With my eyes bulging and my jaw slack in amazement, I stood there and watched helplessly as the hobgoblin stretched himself toward the monster's face...and poked it in the eyes.

The pterosaur screeched, shifting sideways in alarm, and started to dive.

I screamed as the giant dinosaur plummeted toward the ground, already anticipating having to collect Hobs' tiny broken body.

Narina hit it with a burst of powerful wind energy.

Hobs did a swan dive off the thing's feathery back and disappeared into the dust being churned up by Narina's wind.

Narina gave the flying dino a final burst of wind that sent it cartwheeling backward to slam into the surface of the lake. The flying dinosaur had barely splashed into the murky water before the long, spiky form of the sea monster breached the silvery surface, the limp pterosaur clutched in its terrifying maw, and slammed back into the lake with its prize.

From the edge of the woods came a faint but happy demand, "Again!"

I turned to find the hobgoblin climbing out of the bush where he'd landed.

Thank the goddess!

I turned to my friends. "I've had enough fun in the jungle. How about we go home?"

"That sounds wonderful," Archie said, gasping as Alice supported him to Tildy. Blood ran down both of his arms. His shirt was in tatters from the pterosaurs' talons.

Wicked's warm weight pressed against my calves. I looked down to find him peering up at me, his gaze soft with love. I gathered him up, burying my face in his fur. "I missed you too, buddy."

Narina handed Alice the clicker. "Would you drive?" she asked.

"Narina?" Archie asked, his voice filled with shock.

She wrapped him in a hug, earning a pain-filled gasp for her troubles. "Sorry, Archie."

He nodded. "You have a lot to explain," he said, though his tone wasn't filled with the censure his words implied.

"Yes," she agreed. "But let's get you home. I believe the sprite will be able to heal you."

The sprite definitely would, I thought as we all gathered around the magical tortoise.

Right before she flayed me alive for leaving her behind.

17

HOLY HALIBUT IN A HUMVEE!

Sebille was sitting at the table in the bookstore with a cup of tea in front of her when Tildy dropped into the center of the space, with us flopping off her sides. Almost as soon as we stopped moving, Hobs and Wicked took off running toward the dividing door, a happy bounce in their steps as if they'd never been gone.

The door magically opened as Wicked approached the door. I'd replaced that lock several times already because it didn't seem to stop anybody.

"That's interesting," Alice said as Fenwald plowed past us with a yowl and dove through the door before it swung closed. "Your cat opens doors?"

I sighed. "I guess he does." I'd suspected as much for months, but that was the first time I'd actually witnessed it.

I glanced at Sebille, who hadn't moved from her chair. My assistant wore an unhappy expression on her narrow, freckled face. She sat with her legs crossed, the red-sneaker-clad foot bouncing agitatedly on the air. "I'm sorry," I told her. "Narina thought it would be best if we left you behind. Just in case."

I didn't look at the sorceress, but I imagined her accusing glare burning my back for throwing her under the Sebille bus.

"And why would that be?" Sebille asked, her tone cold as ice.

"Because there was a better than good chance we wouldn't make it back," Narina said. She moved to stand next to me. When I glanced her way, I was surprised to see hollows in her cheeks that hadn't been there before.

"She was right," Alice said, grudgingly. "We barely made it out of there alive."

Sebille's gaze never left mine. She didn't care what any of them said. She was mad at me. I was the one who'd left her a note and snuck out of Croakies in the wee hours of the morning. I was the one who'd left her behind. "I'm sorry," I told her. "I know it was a dirty trick to sneak out like that. But I didn't want to leave Croakies without someone to care for it and the artifacts. I wanted that someone to be you. The artifacts trust you. I..." I swallowed hard. "I trust you."

Her expression softened. But, when she stood, her movements were brisk and stiff. "You're buying dinner for a week. And I want donuts every morning for the rest of this month."

I sighed but nodded. "Deal."

She finally shifted her hostile gaze from me. "Archie?"

The question in her tone brought his head up. "Pterosaur claws. Quite a nasty set of them, I'm afraid."

Sebille nodded, motioning toward the chair she'd just abandoned. "Sit. Let me see what I can do."

I also pointed toward the table. "Alice, Narina, sit. I'll bring tea and see what I can scrape up for you to eat."

Alice was so weary she didn't even argue about me making the tea. My tea always tasted like somebody's badly fertilized lawn, with a side of char. But it would do the trick. "I think I have an apple and a peach from Lea's orchard in my kitchen upstairs."

The fruit from Lea's orchard, which was tended by Sebille's mom, Queen Sindra, and her fae subjects, was massively oversized, sweet, and crisp. Each piece of fruit was big enough to feed four people with normal hunger. I'd need something extra for the group of half-starved jungle dwellers.

"You only have an apple," Sebille said, throwing me a glare. "I ate your peach in a fit of righteous anger. It was delicious." Every word was super-charged with rage—each one pinging against my skin like a tiny dart.

I bit back a sigh. I'd be paying for leaving Sebille behind for a very long time. "I'll run out and get us something later," I said meekly.

Sebille sniffed.

It was a relief to put tea in front of my three fellow travelers and disappear upstairs. Sebille hadn't been lying. There was a carefully stripped peach pit on a plate in the center of my kitchen table. The apple was sitting next to it on the plate, untouched.

I sliced the crisp fruit into thin slivers that were six inches long apiece and arranged them on a clean plate. Pulling slices of my favorite cheese from my nearly empty refrigerator, I arranged them on a second plate and grabbed a box of crackers, dumping a pile of them in the center of the cheese plate.

Feeling good about my impromptu offering, I headed back downstairs. The front door jangled softly as I came into the bookstore. Grym came into the store. His eyes caught mine and he gave me a warm smile. That smile did funny things to my stomach. Stumbling slightly, I nearly dropped the two plates.

Grym hurried forward and grabbed an arm to steady me, his gaze narrowing. "You look like you've been run ragged. Are you on a job? I've been trying to catch you for two days. You didn't answer your phone, and the store's been closed." He frowned. "I was worried."

Guilt ate a path through my chest. "Sorry. Yeah, we've been on a particularly brutal job." My eyes slid to Tildy, who, of course, was happily chewing something. There was a pile of fresh lettuce leaves and some strawberries on the carpet in front of her.

Sebille had fed the tortoise for me.

Grym nodded, gently squeezing my arm. "I'm glad you're safe."

My gaze got caught on his and I didn't have the strength to pull it away. Warmth slid through me. My knees knocked together a little. We hadn't seen much of each other since he'd kissed me for the very first time. That kiss had changed things between us. But I wasn't sure exactly how yet. And we hadn't made an opportunity to talk about it.

"Did you bring food?" Alice asked, her voice sounding weak.

I shook myself out of my daze. She and Archie had to be starving. "Yes. Sorry." I smiled at Grym and walked around him, placing the plates on the table.

Archie and Alice dug in like they were ravenous. Even Narina made a tidy sandwich with a piece of cheese and an apple slice, eating it with relish.

"I'm assuming the job had something to do with this tortoise?" Grym walked over and stared down at

Tildy. "Hello there," he said, grinning. "She's a beauty." He glanced at me. "Magical?"

I nodded.

"What does she do?"

"Um..."

"Never you mind, Detective," Alice said grumpily. I was glad to hear that her voice had strengthened. The food and tea were doing their job.

Grym winked at me and I grinned. "No worries, Alice Keeper," he said. "I won't hurt the artifact." He crouched down and eyed the segments of Tildy's colorful shell. "I've never seen anything quite like her." He leaned closer and stretched his hand toward the tortoise's shell before I realized what he was doing. "These runes on her shell are fascina..."

"No!" I yelled as his finger neared the turtle.

He touched a segment of Tildy's shell. Just like that, the two of them disappeared into thin air.

"Holy halibut in a Humvee!" I yelled, rushing over to the spot where the turtle had been. I skimmed a horrified glance toward Alice. She sighed, shaking her head, and punched a button on the clicker.

Tildy and Grym returned in a wash of pine-scented air. Tildy had a mouthful of prickly green branch, and my favorite detective was looking a bit shell-shocked. His dark hair stuck up in strips, the silky strands pasted together with something that had to be sticky because there were pine needles glued to the clumps. His cheeks were covered in dirt, and his shirt hung from him in tatters. Once the sweet scent of pine wafted away, another, much less pleasant smell saturated the space around him.

"Ugh!" I covered my nose. "What is that stench?"

Still looking a bit dazed, Grym slowly looked down at his shoes, grimacing at the mess of leaves stuck to the bottom of one of them. Something thick and brown oozed out from beneath the leafy covering. "I think I stepped in bear scat."

"I say, young man!" Archie exclaimed. "Do remove yourself from the room. Your stench is nearly enough to put me off my food."

Sliding a look toward the now empty plates of food, I raised my eyebrows. "Unless you were going to munch on my plates, I think you were done eating."

Archie shrugged, humor glinting in his blue gaze.

"Never mind the scat," Grym said, grinning. "I saw the coolest castle. It was black."

Narina jumped up and hurried over to Grym. To our collective shock, she grabbed his arm, seemingly oblivious to his stench. "Tell me where you were?"

Grym focused a surprised look on her. "What?"

She tugged a sleeve tatter, her pretty face filled with tension. "Where did you go just now?"

He reached up and scrubbed a hand over his jaw, the sound of whiskers that hadn't been there when he'd left prickling the silence. "I..." He frowned. "I'm not sure."

Narina dropped his arm and tangled her fingers together as if trying to keep herself from shaking him. "Please! It's vitally important."

Grym's intelligent gaze finally sharpened. "I landed in a copse of evergreen trees."

We all looked at the tortoise, who always seemed able to scavenge her next meal, no matter where she ended up.

"Where was it?" Narina's voice cracked. She seemed to be at the end of her control.

Grym shook his head, and I thought he was going to tell her he didn't know again. But he looked thoughtful. "We landed too close to a bear cub, whose mother took exception to my presence there." He glanced at his tattered shirt. I realized he'd been wearing a sports coat when he'd popped away. "I barely got out of there with my life. I ran. By the time I got away from the bear, I'd traveled probably a mile or two through the woods. I ended up on the edge of a cliff, looking down..." His gaze turned thoughtful again. He seemed to be remembering something he'd seen.

"What?" Narina urged, her hand on his arm again. "Tell me what you saw."

"Like I said, it was a castle. Black, with pointy spires that rose into charcoal gray cloud cover." He frowned. "It was strange because the clouds only seemed to hover over the castle."

Narina grabbed his arm with both hands and shook it, leaning into him with wild eyes. "How many spires?"

"Three. Why...?"

Quick as a wink, Narina turned and threw out her hand. A gust of wind smacked into Alice, ripping the clicker from beneath her hand on the table.

Before I could even register what was happening, Narina threw herself onto Tildy, and they disappeared in a puff of evergreen-scented air.

18

CRISPY CRAWFISH CRACKERS!

"Y ou need to think!" Alice yelled at Grym, her round face nearly purple. "She can't be allowed to steal that artifact!"

Grym's jaw tightened to granite. The man was a gargoyle. He knew how to do rock. "Calm down," he told her, crossing his muscular arms over his broad chest. The tatters of his shirt blew in the backdraft of Alice's frantic pacing.

"Alice, take a deep breath..." I said in a soothing voice.

She rounded on me, her beady eyes wild. "She'll kill her!"

"Why do you think Narina will kill the beastie?" Archie asked in his most reasonable voice. "She's actually quite fond of the magical tortoises."

Alice blew air through her lips. "You don't know

her. You never did. She's capable of horrible things when she's...motivated."

I chewed on the inside of my bottom lip, uncomfortable with Alice's statement on several levels. I'd felt a bit unsure of Narina's motives. I could admit that to myself. But I'd also sensed that she was trying to help. "Motivated by what?" I asked. "She told me she was trying to rescue someone."

Alice and Archie shared a look. Archie's expression was filled with warning.

"That's just not true," Archie said, ignoring my question. Anger tightened his voice. "She's only ever had Ed...um...people's best interests in mind. She came back to the jungle for us, didn't she?"

"Why do you suppose she did come for us?" I asked them. "I mean, the first time." I knew what Narina had told me, but I wasn't sure I believed her.

"I assure you it was a mistake," Alice said, glaring at Archie. "She must have hit *Recall* rather than programming in her intended destination."

A flush reddened Archie's cheeks. He glanced at me. "I'm certain she intends no harm to come to the beast."

Alice stopped in front of Archie, her eyes blazing. She poked a pudgy digit into his chest. "You're a fool, Archibald Pudsnecker. You always romanticized him...pretended he was harmless. But he wasn't harmless, was he? He caused no end of trouble for your family, and look what he did to the girl!"

I blinked as they all turned to me. "Huh? What?" Suddenly the subject had changed, and I seemed to be the only one who didn't know what they were talking about. Except for Grym. But he was busy trying to pry the strands of his hair apart. I was pretty sure he wasn't following along.

"What girl? What are you two talking about?" I asked.

Alice just shook her head. Whipping around, she advanced on Grym again. The pudgy assault digit came up and zeroed in on his very nice pecs.

Lightning fast, Grym's hand snapped up and he captured her wrist before the digit could land. "Stop it, Alice Parker. Back up. And let me tell you what I know." He glanced my way. "And then you're going to tell Naida what you were talking about. Because, whatever you're discussing, it sounds like she has a right to know about it."

Huh. Apparently, he hadn't been *totally* distracted by his glued hair.

I was torn between gratitude for his taking up for me and irritation that he thought I needed his help. I glared at Archie. "You and I had this discussion. I understood that my father was dead, and my mother was alive. So who is this Ed-um you're talking about?"

Archie shook his head. "This isn't the time or place..."

I put my hands on my hips. "This is the *only* time. The perfect place."

He sighed. "Your da is dead. I didn't lie to you. He was my best friend and I'll mourn him until I follow him to death."

Alice blew a raspberry. Clearly, she hadn't liked my father. I didn't care. What bothered me more was that both she and Archie had known who my parents were all along, and neither of them had bothered telling me during those first, tumultuous days of my training.

"Then who is this Ed-um guy?" I asked angrily.

Archie walked over and took my hands, squeezing my fingers in his warm grip. His gaze was earnest, slightly sad, but kind. "I have done you a great disservice," he told me. He glanced at Alice, his gaze narrowing in warning. "We all have. And I'll make it right. I'll tell you everything. You have my word. But Alice is right about one thing. Right now, we need to find Narina. I fear she's put herself in great danger, and we need to help her." He lowered his head, speaking softly. "She's only trying to save her son."

"By handing over that beautiful miracle of magic to a monster!" Alice yelled.

It didn't seem possible, but somehow she'd turned even more purple than before.

I held Archie's gaze for a long moment, trying to read the intent in his eyes. I believed him. He would tell me what I wanted to know. So, I nodded. "Okay." Turning to Grym, I asked, "Do you have any idea where you were?"

He tugged on his tattered shirt. "I've been thinking about it, and I believe I do." He slid Alice a tense glance. "I think the castle I saw was in the Enchanted Forest."

Crispy crawfish crackers!

Alice deflated, falling heavily into a chair. "Goblin goobers."

Archie shook his head. "We'll never find it in the forest."

I didn't disagree. I looked at Grym, my gaze pleading.

He gave me a slight smile. "Actually, I believe I know right where it is."

The thing about the Enchanted Forest was that it was magical. That might seem like an obvious statement given the name, but the thing about magical stuff is that it's inherently volatile. And, in the case of the forest, changeable in a very frustrating way.

We stood in a clearing about a mile off the road where we'd parked Grym's big car. The forest rustled and swayed and sang around us. The wind that had been strong enough to blow my long brown hair into my face as we'd left Croakies was a gentle caress within the forest. It wove throughout the many trees, sent leaves and sparkling particles of magic prancing on the air, and provided a steady soundtrack for the song and dance of the millions of creatures living there.

Alice was still wringing her hands and Archie was trying to appear unconcerned, but I saw the tightening around his eyes and the stiffness with which he held himself.

I thought I understood why Alice was upset but had no idea why Archie was so worried. He kept throwing me looks as if he expected me to combust.

Grym was looking up at the sky, his large form motionless.

We'd driven the winding roads of the Enchanted Forest for over an hour before he'd abruptly slowed and pulled his car onto a narrow overlook. Then we'd walked for another hour, Grym changing directions several times, until I'd started to wonder if we hadn't passed through the same areas several times.

Grym had kept his head down and hadn't spoken since leaving the car. He hadn't rushed or slowed. Instead, he'd moved with steady purpose, seemingly intent on the search for the right spot. He'd finally stopped unexpectedly in the very spot where we stood.

He'd been staring off into the distance for the last fifteen minutes, his gaze seemingly on the distant line of mountains.

I was losing hope that he knew where he was. Plus, Alice and Archie were tensing me out.

"Anything?" I asked.

"I need to get higher." He said, eyeing the nearest tree, which happened to be one of the tallest of the billions of trees in the nearby forest.

I knew he was probably wondering if the highest branches would hold him. He didn't look it, but he was really heavy. A rocky magical form would do that to a guy.

"No worries," Alice said. She reached into the rat's nest of her brown hair and plucked Oliver from its depths. "Do your thing, darling," she told the pop-eyed little guy, settling him onto a lower branch.

"What does he do?" Grym asked, looking unconvinced.

"Just wait a tick," Alice told him.

We watched the bright green frog start up the side of the tree, his orange toes easily gripping the chunky bark as he did a combination climb-hop-climb until he disappeared into the uppermost branches.

Alice stared at the tree well after he'd disappeared, her lips curving in a secret smile. "There you are, my lovely." She nodded her bushy head. "Yes, yes."

I shared a confused glance with Grym. When Alice had been "training" me, she hadn't really known what Oliver could do. She'd said something about him "telling" her what he saw in a given instance, but as far as I knew, Oliver couldn't talk. At least not like Mr. Slimy.

Maybe he spoke in pictures?

Alice finally glanced toward Grym. She motioned him over. "Come." She patted her shoulder. "Put your hand here."

Grym didn't hesitate. Although I hadn't been invited, I placed my hand on her other shoulder. I gave a small start of fear as the world inside my head swooped downward in a dizzying wash.

"Uh!" I yelled, letting go of Alice's shoulder.

She laughed happily. "It can be a bugger the first time."

Grym's expression turned intense. "Yes, there's the spot. Right there."

Alice nodded. "Olly, show us the path."

I placed my hand back onto Alice's shoulder and tensed as the view slid away from the plunging drop into a valley, and refocused on a narrow ledge clinging to the death-defying cliff face.

I sucked in a gasp as we visually descended the dizzying heights and then relaxed as we skimmed quickly over the grassy plain below. But as we began to climb again, seemingly heading back into the mountains that rose to snowy peaks far across the forest, my chest tightened again.

Moments later, the midnight husk of a terrifying structure rose into view. The structure appeared to be hewn from acres of black granite, the unwelcoming façade rising in harsh lines from the wide flat ground where it was perched.

Three peaks rose from its long profile, spearing the sky in exact duplicates of the mountain peaks rising behind them. From the conical roof of each daunting peak, a single black and white flag rippled in the hot summer breeze.

I felt Grym tense beside me at the sight of those flags, a husky swear escaping from between his lips.

"Is it her?" Archie asked, stepping forward.

Grym sighed. "Yes."

"Is it who?" I asked. Once again, I was the only one who didn't seem to know what was going on.

Grym lifted his hand from Alice's shoulder and looked at me. "Her name is Dacara," he said. "A very dangerous dual sorceress. I didn't put two and two together when I first saw the castle. But then I remembered her trial and her subsequent..." He seemed to be considering what word to use. "Banishment was the term they used. I'm not sure it's the right word for her situation."

I frowned. "Dual sorceress? What does that mean?"

"You're such a newbie," Alice said, looking disgusted.

I bit back an angry retort. If Alice had trained me like she was supposed to, maybe I might have known more.

"She's a very rare sorcerer who has not one but two legacy magics," Sebille said, frowning. She looked at Grym. "My mother went up against her once. She provided the magic fire to destroy Toad Stool City."

I felt my eyes go wide. "I thought the Quillerans did that."

"With her help, they did," Sebille agreed. "Dacara and Margot Quilleran went to school together. They were best friends. Dacara gave Margot the fire to torch Mother's queendom as a favor." She curled her lip. "But I'm sure it pleased her to do it."

"Yes," Archie agreed. "She's a foul one."

"And you think that's where Narina went?"

"I know it," Archie said, sighing. "Dacara has always had a thing for Eddie. We knew it would end badly."

We stood in tense silence for a long moment. When I couldn't take it anymore, I expelled air. "Well, okay. I guess we'd better get going then."

Everyone looked at me, a variety of emotions on their faces. Grym looked curious. Archie surprised.

And Alice...well...Alice looked slightly green around the gills.

"You want to face off with the dual sorceress?" Sebille asked, her expression neutral.

I shrugged. "That's what we're here for, right? Besides, we faced off with a T-Rex, those really scary bitey dinosaurs that shrieked, the horrible Spiny, and those flying, pointy-headed things. What's one sorceress with a fiery temper after all that?"

Archie's smile was grim. "How could we dispute such a scientifically accurate portrayal of the situation?"

I was pretty sure he'd just dissed me, but I shrugged. "Right?"

19

DIFFERENT JUNGLE...SAME NIGHTMARE

W hy was I continually forced to repeat my worst nightmares?

Once again, I found myself clinging to the side of a cliff, muscles locked in terror, with everyone else standing down below looking up at me with pity...or mocking amusement...at my inability to navigate the vertical abyss on my own. Even with their backpacks weighing them down, everyone but me had easily scampered down the narrow path jutting from the cliff face.

Clearly, I was *special*.

"Come on, Naida," Sebille said in a disgusted tone.

I just knew she was giving her eyes a workout. I could feel her disdain like a pinch against my skin.

"You can do it, child," Archie said, his pep talk

having lost some of its enthusiasm over the last several grueling minutes.

"Come on then, Naida Keeper. Don't be a wanker. You're fully capable of climbing down that pathway just like the rest of us." Amazingly, Alice's usual compassionate teaching methods did *not* soothe my jitters.

"Just don't look down," Grym said, his tone a warm caress against my nerves. "The path is plenty wide enough for you to descend."

I slid sideways a few inches, jolting to a stop when the edge of the narrow path broke away under my foot, rock dust skittering down the cliff face with a soft ping.

Terror clutched me. "Why do we always have to cling to cliffs to do everything?" I whined unattractively.

A collective sigh painted the air at the bottom of the cliff.

A moment later, rock clacked against rock, and I pressed myself closer to the wall as the precipice I was clinging to shifted. "What's going on?" I asked, afraid to look down. "Is the wall crumbling?"

A hard, warm hand touched my side and I recoiled, shrieking as my panic unbalanced me and peeled me away from the wall.

Déjà vu slammed over me again. Unlike before, I wouldn't have a gentle, long-necked dinosaur to break my fall. Instead, I had a hard but surprisingly pliant chest and muscular arms to stop my downward spiral.

I clung to Grym like a drowning victim clings to anything that will help her float. "Oh my goddess, oh my goddess, oh my goddess..." I chanted against his warm throat.

The heavy arm that was wrapped around my waist tightened and a deep, gravelly voice murmured into my ear. "You're okay, Naida. I've got you."

I nodded as panic still swirled through me. Grym might have me, but he had to be barely clinging to the cliffside, and my weight would surely overbalance us if I moved the wrong way.

I stopped nodding in the midst of that terrifying thought. "I'm sorry, I'm sorry, I'm sorry," I chanted instead.

"Don't be sorry," he said, warm breath tickling the side of my throat.

His big body shifted, and a terrifying scratching sound made me tense.

"Oh!" I yelled, burying my face more deeply into his throat.

He shifted again. There was more scratching. And, unbelievably, we moved quickly downward. After a moment, I dared a glance past Grym and discovered the ground was only about ten feet away from us.

I sucked air into lungs that had stopped working somewhere up around thirty vertical feet.

With the loss of fear came the blossoming of physical awareness. I inhaled Grym's scent, finding it clean and slightly woodsy with a hint of pine needles. I'd expected a rockier scent. Then I remembered the glued strands of his hair after his encounter in the evergreens with the mama bear.

His firm body held me close. Really close. And I could admit to myself that his big frame felt good against mine. Solid, strong, and deliciously warm.

By the time Grym stepped down onto the ground, my cheeks had heated with the embarrassment of my un-platonic thoughts.

He set me on my feet, but I was still clinging to him like a pet monkey. My grip was relentless.

"You can let go now, Naida," he murmured, his hands gripping me around the waist as if to pry me loose.

"Mmm," I said, my body locked into immobility.

"Really, Naida," snarled Sebille. "This is embarrassing."

I just barely kept from sighing. After all the terror I'd felt a few moments earlier, the pleasure of feeling safe and...safe...we'd just leave it at that...was intoxicating. "I'd like to stay here a few more minutes," I murmured.

Grym's big frame juddered and I felt the deep timbre of his chuckle beneath my ear. "Okay, but you're going to get a shock when I change back to human."

His laughing threat had me flying backward away from him with a shriek.

Grym stood with his hands on his narrow, rock-like hips and laughed. His wide, handsome face softened under a smile. "I figured that would move you." He turned away and headed toward a tree whose trunk was wide enough to drive my car through, disappearing behind it.

He reappeared a couple of minutes later, fully clothed and back to normal.

Pity. I kind of liked his gargoyle form.

"Where to now?" Archie asked the cop.

Grym pointed toward the rounded hills that looked to be a quarter of a mile away. The foothills. From where we stood, I could just make out the very tops of the black castle's spires, the black and white flags whipping energetically from their peaks. "That way." He frowned. "I'm afraid we aren't going to make it to the castle before dark. We'll camp at the base of the mountain and make our way up in the morning."

As much as I hated the idea of camping inside the enchanted forest, I hated the idea of climbing that mountain in the dark even more.

Or...you know...climbing it at all.

On the other hand, I thought as I fell in behind Grym and the others, maybe Grym would have to rescue me again.

Something to look forward to.

D ifferent jungle...same nightmare.

I huddled against another massive tree, whose uppermost branches were so far over our heads they seemed to disappear into the clouds. Sebille's whistle-snore sawed the night about thirty feet away, near the fire. And, though I would have really liked to stay close to that fire, I needed to put some distance between me and the nerve-jangling sound.

Alice was restless on the opposite side of the fire, but her occasional snore-puffs told me she mostly slept too.

Archie lay a few feet away from the fire as if he'd gotten too hot, his form unmoving and totally silent beneath his sleeping bag. He slept with his arms crossed over his chest like a corpse laid out for viewing.

I shuddered at the thought.

Grym had offered to keep watch for the first half of the night. He'd gotten up and left the clearing a few minutes earlier, probably to circle the perimeter looking for danger.

I'd tried for a couple of hours to sleep but had given up after the last of several screeching cries split the night. As I'd noticed in the wild and wooly Jurassic era, nature was a cruel B-eye-itch, and I wasn't nearly man enough to deal with it.

All that horrifying killing and screaming.

I shuddered again, then flinched away as something flew out of the darkness, heading directly for my face. I got a brief look at a small, fanged face and glowing green eyes before I swung my hands and shooed the nasty little thing away. "You don't scare me," I told it with false bravado. "I've peed my pants over much bigger things than you."

High above my head, an owl called a warning about our presence, its call a haunting lullaby that hung on the air for a full minute after it stopped, weaving through the trees and morphing into the sound of rustling leaves. It was a four-dimensional experience that feathered over my flesh, dulled my hearing, and sent a chill up my spine before it died completely away. I could even smell the sour scent of fear wafting through the trees with the warning sound.

I caught a glimpse of the owl as it lifted from the tree and it was terrifying, with a black body, a white face, and strange white markings over the length of its body that made it look skeletal against the moonlit sky.

Strange, enchanted critters scurried along the ground nearby, their extra-long claws scratching against the dirt and their oversized eyes glinting demonic red in the firelight.

I was really glad we'd decided against bringing

Wicked and Hobs. There was probably no end of trouble they could have gotten up to in that forest.

My eyes drifted closed a moment later, heavy with weariness. Unfortunately, my brain wouldn't stop yammering and let me sleep.

I leaned my head against the rough bark of the tree and sighed, wishing I could just drift away so I wouldn't be a zombie when the fit hit the shan on the following day.

The jungle was silent around me, a warm breeze wrapping me in a comfortable bubble that finally allowed my muscles to relax. I sighed, my muscles heavy. The world turned charcoal around the edges, and I finally felt myself sliding into sleep. I dreamed of jungles and enormous predators, and running, running, running...

Sssssssssss!

The sound was like air leaving a balloon. I wound it into my dreams and slept on, embracing the brightly-hued birthday balloons floating over the face of our cave from the land of the dinosaurs.

Sssssssssss!

It didn't seem strange to have birthday balloons in the jungle. Any more than it seemed strange to see a small dinosaur carrying one around with a string in its mouth.

Dreams are weird.

Sssssssssss!

The escaping air filtered across my face, and I

waved a hand in annoyance. "Can somebody please plug that hole?"

Naida?

In my dream, Grym's voice was soft, filled with warning.

Sssssssssss!

A cool touch glided over my arm, pressing heavily against my skin. The pressure spread and built, tightening to the point of discomfort.

Sssssssssss!

Naida! Wake up.

Why did Grym sound so upset? I shifted in my dream-cave, several balloon strings clutched in my fingers.

Sssssssssss!

Suffocating Snake Sssuspenders! Why won't somebody plug that hole?

Naida!

My chest was heavy. So heavy. All the air had left my lungs and I couldn't breathe. Prickly bark pressed painfully into my back. I tried to move, tried to blow air into a deflating red balloon, but nothing would come.

Sssssssssss!

"Naida!"

I jolted awake. My eyes shot open and I saw Grym. He was standing several feet away with a knife clutched in his hand. His gaze was locked on something below my chin.

I opened my mouth to ask him what...and realized I couldn't draw air.

Panic sliced through me. I tried to jerk away from the tree and discovered I couldn't move.

Sssssssss!

My vision swam, my head felt like it was going to explode, and my arms and legs had gone numb.

Something thick and cool slid over my skin, coiling, tightening.

I tried to scream, but nothing would come out. There was no air.

Goddess, why was there no air!

"Do something!" Archie barked out.

Sebille hovered near Grym, her gaze lit with rage. "We can't."

Alice's round face was pale in the firelight, her small eyes rapidly blinking. "What's happening! What is that thing that's wrapped around Naida?"

Sssssssss!

"I hate this stupid forest," Sebille growled out.

Grym's gaze never left mine. Amazingly, though I couldn't draw air, somehow I didn't suffocate. I was uncomfortable for sure. Unable to move. But my thoughts were clear, and I wasn't passing out.

"It's injected her with venom," Grym said. "Even if we get it off her, she'll die without an antidote."

"Where in the name of the goddess's best Tupperware are we going to get that?" Alice asked.

Archie came up beside Grym. His hands planted

on his narrow hips, he looked at me as if I were a science experiment. The void sorcerer appeared more fascinated than horrified.

"It's in the fangs," Archie said, nodding as if he'd just recalled an intriguing piece of scientific evidence. "This species harbors a duality."

"Explain!" Grym growled.

Yeah, Archie, please explain! I screamed in my head. It wasn't nearly as satisfying as screaming outside my head. But it was all I had at the moment.

"Duality," he repeated as if we were all dense for not understanding. When he was met with four blank gazes, he sighed.

Okay, to be fair, it was two blank gazes (Alice and me); one gaze that promised a serious throttling if he didn't spill something helpful soon (Grym); and one that threatened he was about to spend the rest of his days as a worm, procreating with himself.

I don't think I need to tell you who that last one came from.

"It's a fascinating creature, actually," Archie began, then turned as white as my wide backside when Grym growled and clenched his fists. "It's very simple, really..."

"Archie!" Alice screamed.

"Okay, okay." Archie shook his head, disgusted that we weren't as enthralled by the scientific intrigue represented by my attacker as he was. "It has one set of fangs that injects the venom and one set that injects the anti-venom."

"So, all we need to do is let it bite her again?" Sebille asked, looking much too comfortable with the idea of my getting bitten a few more times.

The sprite holds a grudge.

I tried to fire hatred and warning at her with my eyes, but I was pretty sure all I did was drool.

Archie frowned. "Of course, it's not that simple."

Of course.

"We need to figure out which set of fangs is the venom and which is the anti-venom. If we choose wrong, the second dose of venom will surely kill her."

Well, wasn't that just a frog-flipping foray into the ferking funhouse?

20

DUALITY'S A MOTHER FLUFFER!

"Amphisbaena," Archie said almost cheerfully. "I've read about them, of course, but I had no idea they were this large."

Sebille glared around the forest. "It's this stupid forest. Everything inside it is dangerous and cranky."

She should fit right in, I thought uncharitably. Then I felt guilty for the thought. She actually looked worried about me. I hadn't known she'd cared. Besides, with me gone, there would be no remaining witnesses to her girlish shrieking when the T-Rex invaded our hidey-hole and threatened to eat us.

The thought gave me pause. She wouldn't...? Would she?

Nah. Maybe.

Help!

I tried to swallow, but nothing moved. The heavy

stench of reptile filled my nostrils and panic sliced my gut into ribbons. *Snakes.* I hated snakes.

A twig snapped behind me and the thing that was clamped around my chest reared up with a hiss.

Baked Banshee beans! I thought as I caught my first sight of the thing holding me hostage.

It had a wide, flat head with massive fangs that glistened wetly as it hissed at whatever was trying to sneak up on it. Its eyes were a sickly bright yellow, the slanted pupils flaring with rage as it struck out at the intruder.

Heavy footsteps retreated as the snake's head snapped back, its long black tongue tasting the air.

"You need to keep it alive," Archie called out as the footsteps approached again.

"Got it," said a deep, gravelly voice I recognized all too well.

Grym!

No, no, no, no, no! I didn't want him to get bitten too. I had to shake off whatever the snake's venom had done. I had to stop him!

A stick appeared in my peripheral vision, smacking the snake in the head.

The thing hissed again and struck, its fangs piercing the wood as if it were butter.

The stick retreated, glossy with venom.

"Got the first sample," Grym announced.

Without warning, the snake's long body began to unwind. It happened so quickly I barely saw it happen. The second head whipped into view and the thing shot forward, flying through the air toward where Grym presumably stood.

No!

My brain told me to jump to my feet and help Grym. My body said, "Oh, heck no. You're just going to sag slowly sideways until your face hits the dirt."

Hello? I glared silently at the threesome standing uselessly ten feet away. *Did you forget something? Or someone?*

"Keep track of which end is which!" Sebille screamed at Grym.

There was a meaty whacking sound, which I hoped was Grym smacking the snake and not the other way around.

"Can't you stun it or something?" Alice asked Sebille. The former Keeper's beady eyes bugged, her fingers twisting with nervous agitation.

"Ah!" Grym screamed behind me.

I concentrated hard and managed to move one foot a quarter of an inch. It was enough to shift a skinny twig on the ground and catch Archie's attention. His distracted gaze slid my way.

Archie flinched, his eyes going round. "Oh! Naida's free. We need to move her..."

Sebille waved a hand and I flew toward them, slamming into Archie and Alice and sending them to the ground with me.

Ouch...

Sebille rolled her eyes. "Stupid forest. It amplifies everything..." Her eyes widened as she had a thought. Then she screamed. "Grym, make your skin harder. Become your rock."

"Arrrghhh!" he responded.

There was more thrashing and hissing and the sound of rocks being thrown. Hopefully not *Grym's* rocks... No, no, forget I thought that. Wipe it from your mind.

I really wished I could see what was going on. I glared at Archie because he was the only one in my line of sight. Well...except for Sebille, but she was ignoring me as usual.

Archie's gaze stumbled over mine, and he flinched. "What? Why are you glaring at me?"

Help. Him. I thought fiercely at the addle-headed sorcerer.

"Huh? Oh." He turned to Alice. "I say, I think she wants us to help the gargoyle."

"There's no bloody way I'm getting' anywhere near that beast," Alice declared.

Archie frowned. "There's no need to be coarse. And besides, what's wrong with Grym?"

I could almost hear Alice roll her beady eyes. "I wasn't talkin' about the gargoyle, ya wanker. I abhor snakes with *one* head." She shuddered. "You're not getting me anywhere near a snake with two fanged ends."

"That's it, now grab both ends..." Sebille instructed.

"Sprite, if you don't stop barking orders at me..." Grym said, leaving her to imagine the rest of his threat.

Sebille rolled her eyes again. "Just trying to be helpful, gargoyle."

"If you want to be helpful...ugh! Ah!" Grym lost the thought for a beat while he seemingly whacked on the snake some more. "Then get your narrow butt over here and smack this thing with some magic. It moves too fast for me to grab, and I've got about a hundred fang marks in my rock."

Fang marks! My poor heart sped in panic. I fed my fear into my eyes and beamed it at Archie.

He patted me on the shoulder. "No worries, Naida girl. He's a gargoyle. They're magically impervious to most types of venom. His hide's so hard and thick it can't get to him. He'll be fine."

"Arrrghhh!!!"

"Sssssssssss!"

Okay, that was it. I couldn't move my body, but my magic didn't need movement to take hold. Concentrating as hard as I could, I gathered my keeper magic and forced it out in a wash of silvery energy. It hit the air with a soft boom, knocking Sebille, Archie, and Alice off their feet and sending them skidding across the clearing on their backsides.

Oops!

Sebille wasn't kidding. The Enchanted Forest really did magnify magical energy.

Behind me, the battle stilled for a heartbeat and then resumed.

I waited anxiously for a long moment but nothing answered my magic. *Dang a Doppelganger's double digits!* I'd blown my friends up for nothing.

Finally, a soft throbbing filled the air high above our heads. I would have stiffened with fear if I hadn't already been magically frozen.

I prayed I hadn't called that skeleton owl back. That thing was terrifying.

Thromp, thromp, thromp, thromp.

My heartbeat slowed to match the rhythm of those wings, dread pounding the same painful cadence in my temples.

With an exaggerated groan, Alice pushed upright. "What's that?"

Sebille stood, brushing dirt off her backside and glaring at me.

I tried to look innocent.

Thromp, thromp, thromp, thromp.

Ugh! The tension was killing me. What had I unleashed?

"Caw!"

Oh goddess, no. Not that.

"Caw! Caw!"

Why me?

A large winged shape eclipsed the silver moon high above. Wings spread wide, the flying menace tilted and dove, moonlight shimmering around him like an aura.

I would have given anything to close my eyes and pretend he wasn't there.

"Caw!"

But alas...

The raven sailed into the clearing and landed with a hop, lifting his wings and shivering as he resettled their ruffled edges. He ambled over to me and shivered again, cocking his head and fixing me with a beady silver gaze. When he spoke, it was with a deep voice thick with a Russian accent and bursting with arrogant derision. "Well, it's another fine mess you've gotten yourself into, girl."

Rasputin. Goddess save us all.

21

GODDESS IN A GONDOLA!

"Maybe you could save your criticisms until that two-headed snake is dead," Sebille growled out in response.

"No need to save it." The raven lifted his wings and danced sideways, his feathers once again sifting upward and resettling as he settled his piercing silver gaze on the sprite. "I've got plenty more where that came from." He hopped around as if celebrating his witty response. "I hope you weren't expecting me to do something about *that*." He jerked his beak toward the activity I still couldn't see behind me. "I don't do magical snakes."

Alice stepped forward, shoving her thick-lensed glasses up her pug nose. "Unless I'm mistaken, ya cur, you answered a Keeper's summons. I do believe that makes you a magical artifact."

The raven stuck his beak in the air and danced

from foot to foot. "I am no such thing. As you know, Madeline lives in this forest. She felt the KOA's magic and sent me to find out what was going on." He slid his arrogant gaze to me. "I should have known the ditz would find the forest's only Amphisbaena," he said, laughter in his voice.

My hopes sank. Rasputin wouldn't help us unless somebody forced him to. We were on our own.

Archie lifted his gaze to where the meaty sounds of battle continued. "I say, Detective, how's it going?"

Grym grunted out an indecipherable response.

Sebille rolled her eyes. "I'm going to have to stun it."

The raven flicked its arrogant gaze to the sprite. "That will do you no good, girl. The antidote only works if the snake is awake and aware."

"Whose daft idea was that?" Alice exclaimed in clear outrage.

The bird's "shoulders" shifted in what might have been a shrug. "It's called preservational evolution. If it wasn't so, any neanderthal with magic could just slap the poor thing upside the head...er heads...and milk the anti-venom from it."

"I don't see the problem with that scenario," Sebille said.

"Well, of course not," Rasputin growled. "You're not the snake."

She snorted.

Rasputin lifted his wings. "Well then. I'll be off."

"Don't you dare!" Grym yelled. "If you let the Keeper die, I'll report to Madeline that you made no attempt to help. I don't believe the PTB and the Magical Universe will be thrilled to hear how carelessly you treated their selected Keeper. Do you?"

I was impressed. Grym's voice was breathless from battle, and his words were interspersed with grunts and panting from the fight, but he was right. And he'd found a way to force the stupid raven to help.

As the Power That Be for the earthly dimension, Madeline Quilleran would be displeased with her sidekick if he did nothing and let me die. Not to mention Rustin's cousin, Maude, who considered herself my friend. Neither powerful witch should be trifled with.

Especially not by a raven familiar with relatively little power compared to theirs.

Rasputin lifted his wings again, his beady gaze narrowing with pique. He glared down at me as if wondering if he could "accidentally" beak me in the face.

I tried to glare a promise of retribution back at him.

He snorted dismissively. "Very well."

Rasputin lifted off the ground and flew past me, his wings a soft *Thromp, thromp, thromp* on the air as he lifted skyward. "I'll seize one end," the bird said in an angry monotone. "Do you think you can manage the other end? Or do you expect me to grab both for you?"

"Shut it, bird," Grym grumbled. "I just need help holding it still so I can catch it."

A moment later, the snake erupted in enraged hissing and Grym grunted one last time. "Got you, you spawn from Hades."

Grym's heavy footfalls sounded behind me and, when he came into view, he was holding what looked like a ten-foot snake in his enormous blocky fists. The nasty thing had a head on either end, massive fangs displayed in what I assumed was a warning posture. The middle sagged toward the ground between Grym's enormous feet.

If I hadn't been so horrified (and could move), I'd have giggled at the sight. Grym looked like he was wearing mittens of the kind small children wore, with a string connecting the two so one of them wouldn't get lost.

Ugh! I thought, giving an internal shudder at the idea that I'd had *that* wrapped around me.

Rasputin lifted into the air and took off without another word.

Grym glared at the others, panting. "Now what?"

Archie sighed. "Now we do eenie, meenie, miney, moe and let one end bite me. If I go rigid, we'll know which end is the venom. If I don't, we'll know which end is the anti-venom."

Grym's brows lifted. "And if you go rigid?"

Archie frowned. "I'll survive a second bite. I'm currently trying to convince myself it's a useful scientific experiment. I'll write a paper. It will be fine."

Grym expelled air in a sigh. "Good luck with that." But he approached the void sorcerer with his snake mittens.

I watched in horror as Grym moved close to Archie and, after receiving a nod to go ahead, shoved one end of the horrible reptile toward Archie's outstretched arm.

"Are you sure you don't want to rest for a while?" Grym asked me again.

As I had the previous four times, I shook my head. "I need to keep moving." It was the simple truth. After being locked in distressing immobility under the Amphisbaena's horrible spell, the simple act of walking felt like a blessing.

"Does that still sting?" he asked me, nodding toward my arm.

I glanced down at the angry red bite, grimacing at the memory of the strike. The only thing worse than being completely immobile under threat of death was being immobilized while watching those frightening fangs sink into my flesh. "It's better."

I looked at Archie, who was paler than he should

have been but seemed otherwise fine despite the two bites he'd been forced to take to help me.

I caught his eye and gave him a smile that I hoped even slightly conveyed my gratitude for what he'd done. "I just want to finish what we came to do and get out of this stupid forest," I mumbled.

Grym's big, warm hand wrapped around mine and squeezed in silent understanding. "The path starts just over this last hill." He lifted his gaze toward the black castle clinging to the side of the snow-tipped mountain, about midway up its daunting face.

The castle looked even larger than I expected. A bruise-colored sky hunkered down over it. "This place has its own, built-in gloom," I murmured, my voice soft with dread.

Grym nodded. "Yeah. I'm not really liking the looks of it."

"She's not a storm sorceress," Archie said, frowning.

Grym and I turned to him, and he jerked his chin toward the purple-black sky. Large flying creatures circled above the castle like a bad cliché, their feathers sparking purple-black as they banked and caught thin ribbons of sunlight the overcast sky above them had allowed through. "Dacara," Archie clarified. "The clouds are probably an indirect result of her magic. Residual energy buildup." He shrugged. "It's not really all that surprising if you think about it. Like everything else in the universe, magic is a collection of ions…"

Aaaaand, I tuned him out. Turning to Grym, I asked, "Can we beat her?"

To my surprise, he didn't answer right away. His attention seemed as fixated on those flying things as mine had been.

"Grym?"

He shrugged. "To be honest, I don't know. Everything I've heard about this sorceress is that she's evil beyond compare. She was banished to the Enchanted Forest a century ago and, though many were relieved that her horrible magic would be contained, there was also a lot of concern about what would happen to it within the super-charged magic of the forest." His dark-caramel gaze narrowed. "If just the residual effects are able to change the weather above her castle…" He didn't bother finishing that thought. He didn't need to. It was clear as day.

We were toast. Worse, we were burnt toast crumbs. The ones stuck in the bottom of the toaster, forgotten and reviled, and then carried off by ants and cockroaches to feed even more nasty scavengers.

I shuddered as I realized the totality of what we'd set out to do. And then I tried to remember why exactly we'd set out to do it.

Oh, yeah. Narina.

And who was she to me again? I sighed, knowing

I'd help her even if Archie hadn't really been worried about her. She'd helped us escape the Jurassic era. She needed our help. We would help. I only hoped it wasn't the last thing we ever did.

What did it say about me that I was kind of missing old Spiny?

O ne in a row. The "path" leading up the side of Dacara's mountain was actually wide enough for me to climb without wanting to fold into the fetal position.

Go me.

Two-thirds of the way up, I was actually feeling kind of cocky about things. Despite the heavy cloud cover that turned mid-day to the dark of night, everyone was still in one piece. Nobody had assaulted us as we neared the scary-looking castle. Maybe the tales about Dacara had been exaggerated. Getting taller and taller with each telling, and less real. Maybe old Dacara had become something of an urban legend. She was probably just a nice girl who thought she looked good in black...and had skeleton tattoos. She was probably just misunderstood. Surely she spent her days compiling care packages for those in need around Enchanted.

Yep. That was it.

Dacara was just misunderstood. She and Narina

were likely sitting on the balcony under the storm clouds at that very moment, drinking tea and discussing Dacara's decorating plans for the downstairs half bath. Sure, she'd done most of the castle in midnight hues, relieved only by various shades of gray and blood red, but it was time for a freshening up. Those pentagram rugs had to go. And the lamps that looked like skeletons? Gone. They were so last year.

I chuckled at the thought, taking another step without paying attention and bumping into Alice's backside with an *oomph*!

To my shock, the ex-Keeper didn't turn and give me a nasty look or a verbal lashing. She was staring up at the flying black things above our heads.

I realized with a start that everyone else was staring at them too.

Okay, I'd bite. I lifted my gaze. "What are we looking a..." My teeth clanked together, slicing the rest of my question off before it could emerge fully formed.

I blinked rapidly. The things that had been circling the castle were much closer than the last time I'd looked—scary close. And, was it my imagination, or had they switched to circling us instead of the big black monstrosity above us?

They didn't have wings as we'd thought from a distance. No feathers. No beaks.

Holy mother of monstrous moments! "Are those

what I think they are?" I asked, my voice cracking like a pre-pubescent boy's.

Nobody responded. I really couldn't blame them. I suddenly found it hard to speak too.

I swallowed as fear razored through me, slicing my belly to ribbons. *Gulp!*

We wouldn't even make it to the castle. "Please tell me those aren't wraiths?" I whispered, terror throbbing in my voice.

Goddess in a gondola! We were about to become wraith kibble right there on the side of the mountain.

Since nobody would answer me, I kept talking to myself. "Is it too late to turn tail and run?" I squeaked.

At the head of the line, Grym turned back, his handsome face shadowed in the gray light. I didn't need sunlight to make out his taut jawline and intense expression. With minimal movement, he shifted forward, putting his weight on his leading foot. "We do need to run, but not back. We're closer to the top than the bottom," he said in a harsh whisper. "If they attack us here, we're dead. There's no room to maneuver. We need to get to open ground if we hope to survive."

Grym slid a look in my direction, his eyes blazing in the low light. He seemed to be waiting for me to do something, so I sucked air into my lungs and shifted forward. Then I gave him a tight nod and placed my hand on Alice's back.

A moment later, Grym growled out a single word. "Run!"

I shoved Alice into motion and started running as if my life depended on it. Because it surely did.

22

I REALLY NEED A VACATION

A blood-chilling shriek split the night above us. The shock of the horrible sound made me stumble, bracing myself on Alice's lumbering form before I fell. The first wraith dove toward us, targeting Grym in its headlong rush toward the ledge.

Another ear-splitting shriek tore through the quickly darkening space. My knees gave out under the sound and I fell, dimly aware of Alice and Archie hitting the ground with me. I curled into a fetal position and covered my ears, screaming against the agony piercing my brain.

There was a flash of dark silver light, and I heard Grym grunt.

I uncovered my ears and forced myself to stand, realizing I'd left Grym to bear the brunt of the attack.

Something buzzed past me, emitting a soft green light that pulsed around iridescent wings.

Sebille!

She shot skyward and hit the wraith that was diving toward me, sending a beam of energy into the sky above it and darting away as a silvery energy wrapped the thing in a thick bubble. The wraith clawed at the bubble but couldn't break it.

"Use protective magic only!" she screamed as she shoved the falling wraith, sending it away from us.

I didn't have protective magic. Not really. But maybe the power boost from the forest would help. I yanked my magic forward and thought about forming it into a bubble that covered Alice and Archie too. I would have tried to grab Grym, but he was far ahead of us on the path in his gargoyle form. His clothing hung in tatters, barely clinging to his enormous, blocky form.

That would explain the flash of silver light.

To my shock, the bubble I created was dense and shimmered with opaline light. There were many things I hated about the forest, but its effect on my magic wasn't one of them.

A wraith fell from the sky, its form bent and boneless as it plunged downward...heading right for me.

Without thinking, I stabbed a foot out and slammed it into the thing's side, sending it arcing out over the cliff's edge, toward the distant ground below.

Not waiting to see it hit, I grabbed Alice's arm, giving it a tug. "We need to move. Grym needs our help."

She climbed to her feet, face slack with fear.

"Use your magic," I told her. "It works better here."

She nodded and I glanced at Archie. "You okay?"

He was pale and held himself stiffly, but he nodded. His dark brows lowered. "I'm fine."

"Do what you can do," I told him. Then I slipped past them and started running, energy biting at my fingertips.

A dark shape dove at me from above. So fast. Too fast. I barely had time to fling a bolt of energy in its direction before it was on me, slamming into my body and driving me down to my knees.

Pain lanced through my bones as my knees crashed into rock. I barely noticed it. Long, white claws, as thick as my little finger, clamped onto my shoulders and the thing shoved forward, trying to take me to my back.

Ugly images of death and destruction shot through me, tearing a track through my body with a violence that was fire and ice at the same time.

Agony spread wherever the wraith's magic touched.

I tried to scream but had no breath in my lungs to do it.

I only had time to register the roiling orange eyes and the long slit in its middle gaping open before the thing just winked away.

"Are you okay?" Archie asked, reaching to help me to my feet. I cried out as he pulled me upright, something in my shoulders ripping under the movement.

Warm blood ran from several slices along my skin.

I didn't take the time to look at the claw marks. I started moving again. "What did you do to it?" I asked the sorcerer.

"Sent it to a void," he said, looking positively enraged. "I hate those dung blasted things."

Two more wraiths dove toward us. Archie sent one into a void, and I blasted the other with energy, aiming for that strange opening in the center of its body.

Seeing the strange slit widening in its torso reminded me of a story my friend LeeAnn Mapes had once told me about when she and her witch, Deg, were attacked by wraiths. I couldn't remember the particulars of the attack, only one very important thing.

They drew energy from magic attacks.

Too late, I realized my mistake. The wraith I'd

fired energy into had been momentarily blown away from us. But only for a second.

It seemed to grow before my very eyes, the roiling orange gaze flaring brighter before it shot back in my direction.

"Archie!" I screamed.

The wraith was inches away when it suddenly winked out. I slammed to a stop at the sound of another scream. It wasn't the bone-melting scream of the wraiths.

I spun around to find Alice on the ground, thrashing beneath a wraith that was bigger than any of the others. The wraith's black cloak floated on the air around it, as if it carried its own personal energy field everywhere it went. The thing hovered over Alice with its claws dug deep into her shoulders.

And she was screaming, long and sharp, the sound ripping a piece of my soul away with every shrill note.

It's my fault, I realized in a jolt of sudden understanding. I'd told her to use her power. That was the worst advice I could have given her. It would have only strengthened the thing.

I had to stop it.

I took off running as Archie sent another wraith into the voids. More and more of the things dropped from the sky to attack.

I was focused on Alice, knowing I had to make it right. I had to get that thing off of her before she lost her mind from the black images I was sure it was sending directly into her brain.

I didn't think. Didn't consider what I was about to do. I simply ran, forcing my magic to retreat as I threw back my head and sent a primal scream into the air.

The wraith's head jerked up, its eyes sending dual orange flares into the thickening darkness. There was no face beneath the constantly moving black robes—no features beyond that horrifying gaze. But ice began to claw at my chest. Fire burned along my muscles as I forced myself to leap into the air, letting the impetus of my leap send me crashing against the nasty hovering bug.

To my vast surprise, I hit a solid form.

I was aware of a sharp cry as the wraith's horrible claws were ripped from Alice's plump shoulders, and she lifted off the ground for a beat before folding bonelessly back onto the cool rock.

I had no time to worry about her as the wraith hit the ledge and skidded along the rocky surface, with me riding its disgusting form.

Fire burned my belly and I thought it was magic, then I noticed the wraith's middle was opening, and I realized I had to move. Fast.

Nothing good would come from that horrible opening.

As soon as we stopped sliding, I shoved my toes against the path and pushed myself upward, ducking sideways as the wraith's claws slashed toward my middle. I slammed into the cliff face and bounced off, somehow starting to run even as the wraith lifted effortlessly from the ground.

Ahead of me on the path, green light bathed Alice. I realized Sebille was healing her.

Ice wrapped around my calves, burning and freezing my flesh at the same time. I stumbled, my feet suddenly too numb to feel the ground. "Sebille!" I screamed, falling to my stomach and skidding toward the sprite and her patient.

She shot past me and the burning, numbing ice disappeared as Sebille drew the thing away.

Several yards from the edge of the cliff, the wraith chasing Sebille winked out of sight.

Archie had voided it.

I felt something inside me relax as the glowing green form that was Sebille shot back in our direction.

"Goddess," Alice moaned, still flat on her back.

Heavy footsteps pounded toward us. "Is she all right?" Grym asked in his gravelly voice. I glanced up at him, swallowing hard and nodding. "I think so. Sebille healed her."

"Death. So cold," Alice mumbled, her entire body shuddering and quaking. "Freezing and fire." She cried out and wrapped her arms around herself.

"Physically, anyway," I amended.

"We need to go. We've beaten the watchers back, but Dacara will send more troops soon."

I wanted to cry. More wraiths? I suddenly felt too tired to move. "Maybe Narina doesn't really need rescuing?" My tone was hopeful and filled with weariness.

Grym grinned. The sight warmed and energized me. "Come on, Naida Keeper, you're not giving up, are you? We've been in tough spots before."

Yeah, I thought. *Lots of them. Many of them over the last two or three days.* "I really need a vacation."

Grym grabbed my hand and tugged me off the ground. "Good idea. But first, we just need to fight our way into that castle up there, defeat the evil sorceress, and rescue Narina and whoever she came to save."

"Piece of cake," I panted out, bending over and resting my hands on my knees. I jerked my chin toward Alice, who was still mumbling nonsense and quivering. "What about her?"

Grym picked the former keeper up and settled her gently over one broad shoulder. "Come on, Archie's waiting for us."

I shuddered violently, running my hands over my arms again. The little hairs on the back of my neck had been standing at attention since we'd stepped onto flat ground. A pervasive sense of impending doom twisted my stomach into knots.

After the violence and chaos of the climb to the castle, the grounds leading to the fortress itself were nerve-janglingly quiet. We walked in nervous silence toward the massive front doors, our gazes swinging nervously around the space with every step.

It didn't seem possible for the area to be completely unguarded. Not after what we'd just barely survived.

Sebille buzzed from right to left, front to back, and even far above our heads, looking for trouble. Each time she returned, she gave us a single shake of her tiny head to let us know there was nothing.

Dacara certainly had a bipolar idea of protection.

Visitors will be killed!

Visitors will be ignored.

I could only wonder what would be next. Visitors will be fanned and fed plump, sweet grapes?

"Maybe the wraiths were a test," Alice offered, her expression tight with a mixture of fear and worry.

Grym shook his head. "There's something in the air. I can feel it."

I nodded, not trusting myself to speak. A lump of dread was lodged in my throat.

When we were ten feet away from the doors, something thumped. The sound was shockingly loud in the silence.

We all screeched to a stop.

With a long, strident creak, the massive wooden doors slowly opened into the castle.

I swallowed hard, but the lump in my throat refused to dislodge.

Sebille buzzed quietly beside me, hovering in a soft glow of green light. When I turned my head I found her looking at me, her tiny face filled with intensity. "I'll hang back. If something happens, I'll have more options," she said.

I knew what she was telling me, and it made me tense. If we were captured, Sebille wanted to be free to hopefully release us. It was a good thought. If she stayed in her sprite form, she could travel unseen through the castle. She'd be a good back-up plan. I nodded. "Be careful," I whispered.

Sebille rolled her tiny eyes and shot skyward.

I sighed. The sprite wasn't good with tender emotions. She treated them like everything else. First, she tried to ignore them. If that didn't work, she'd beat them verbally into submission. If neglect and hostility didn't wash the uncomfortable things away, derision was a good last-ditch plan.

A large, warm hand found my back. I looked up

into Grym's human face, ignoring the tatters of his human clothing to examine the long, bloody wound that ran from his shoulder to his flat belly. It looked puffy and angry. "You should have had Sebille heal that," I scolded softly.

He shook his head. "It's fine. I'll deal with it when we get back."

"It looks infected."

"Poison, most likely." He frowned. "Goddess knows what those things had on their claws."

At my look of alarm, he grinned. "It's fine, Naida. Are you ready to go kick evil sorceress butt?"

That surprised a laugh out of me. "Not even a little."

He leaned close and, to my extreme surprise, placed a gentle kiss on my lips. "For luck," he said as he straightened.

My lips tingled, and I smiled despite myself. We were all going to die. But, hey, the kiss was nice.

23

AM I UNDER ARREST, OFFICER?

I was the last one through the door. As it started to creak loudly closed behind me I heard the familiar buzz of a dragonfly-sized sprite shoot by overhead.

I forced myself not to look at Sebille. I had no idea who might be watching us from the shadows. And there were a lot of shadows. Enough shadows, in fact, to hide an entire army of the nasty wraiths from view.

The room we entered was as big as a warehouse, dark and cold. The floor beneath our feet was made of stone blocks. Far above our heads hung a ceiling which was mostly lost to shadow. The only way I knew the ceiling was there, was because I could just make out the soft gleam of a massive chandelier, and it had to be attached to something. But I couldn't tell what any of it looked like. It was too dark.

If it weren't for that floor and ceiling, I would have thought we were still outside. Except that it was colder than it had been out there.

The silence was almost a physical presence in the space, thick and gooey. The air was clammy against my skin.

I wondered how Sebille was going to sneak around if the whole place was as quiet as the one where we stood. Her soft buzzing would sound like a 747 in the silence.

We stood together in a clump beneath the only light in the room. Large sconces made of pitted brass shone from the wall on either side of the heavy doors, bathing a ten-foot by ten-foot space in weak yellow light.

I rubbed my arms, moving closer to Grym's heat, and focused on breathing in and out. The room smelled like mildewed earth and despair. High above us, the shadows shifted and then stilled.

Whispered words, indecipherable despite the quiet, danced through the glooms.

I reached over and clasped Grym's densely muscled arm. "Did you hear that?" I asked as softly as I could and still be heard.

He laid a hand over mine but didn't respond.

In the distance, light flared in a thin, horizontal line that slowly widened. It took me a beat to realize I was watching a door open.

The room beyond the door was bright, highlighting a blazing fireplace on the opposite wall. A small form stood in the center of the open door. The newcomer didn't speak for a long moment and didn't move.

She finally seemed to rouse herself and stepped forward. As she moved into the enormous room, the chandelier high above our heads flared to life, bathing her in a soft light that followed where she walked.

I'd expected something from a fairy tale—a sorceress from an old telling of witches and terrible magic-wielders.

The woman moving toward us was nothing like I'd predicted. She moved with a confidence I would have never expected, given that she looked about eighteen years old. The small woman grinned widely as she neared, her pixie face pale against the spiky cap of her silky black hair. A soft blush touched her sharp cheeks, and her rosebud lips were glossy and pink. Large cross earrings—covered in diamonds if the spark off the overhead lighting was any indication—swayed from delicate ears. "Hello!" she said, grinning widely. "What a nice surprise. I never get visitors."

I blinked at the unexpected greeting, wondering what she was hiding.

"I'm thinking that might be because of the deadly wraiths," Alice said, sniffing with irritation.

The waif in front of us, no taller than five foot

three if I had to guess, looked surprised. Her slender black brows rose into her spiky bangs. "Oh! I'm so sorry. They weren't supposed to bother you without checking with me first." She laughed dismissively. "I'm afraid I was in my workroom. When I start on a project, I tend to lose track of everything."

She stopped in front of us, clasping small hands covered in an abundance of silver rings before her. "Good thing I stopped for lunch, or I might not have known you were here at all." Pleasure lit her small face, and she clapped her hands like a joyful toddler. "You can eat with me. What fun!"

When we just stared at her, she snorted. "Oh. So sorry." She jabbed a hand in my direction. "I'm Dacara. And you are?"

"Friends of Narina's," Archie said on a scowl. He clearly wasn't buying the waif's act.

Alice's chin lifted. "I believe you have a magical artifact that belongs to us."

Dacara's smile never wavered. Instead, amazingly, she clapped her hands again with delight. "My project! Yes. Would you like to see?"

I wasn't at all sure that I would. Judging from the expression that crossed Alice's round face, I didn't think she would either.

But Archie nodded, the scowl firmly entrenched on his face.

Grym reached for Dacara's hand. "Miss Dacara,

I'm Detective Grym, Enchanted Police Department. How are you?"

The tiny sorceress's gaze widened when she took Grym's hand. I was pretty sure her eyes were a dark, dark brown, but they looked black in the shadowed room. "Oh my. Am I under arrest, officer?" She put her hands out in front of her, wrists together as if bound by invisible handcuffs, and winked saucily at Grym.

Something green and ugly flared from the vicinity of my heart. I suddenly didn't like Dacara the dual sorceress. I didn't like her one little bit.

I shoved my hand at her, accepting the handshake she'd offered before. "Dacara, I'm Naida Griffith, Keeper of the Artifacts. I'm here to retrieve Tildy, the magical tortoise. If you'll just show us where she and Narina are, we'll get out of your hair."

The sorceress held my gaze for a long moment, her eyes narrowing just the tiniest bit as if assessing me. Then she laughed gaily. "KOA Griffith, it's quite an honor to meet you." Her glance swung from me to Grym, and the smile widened. "And you came with the long arm of the law." The way she looked Grym over, all but licking her lips with appreciation, made me want to claw her eyes right out of her head.

Yeow! I pulled air into my lungs. I had to get a grip.

"Yes. The Enchanted Police do have an interest in

seeing the tortoise returned to the Keeper for safe...
er...keeping."

Dacara giggled. She spun on her heel, motioning
for us to follow. "Come. I'm sure you're going to love
what I'm working on. Follow me."

Though I would rather have followed Spiny to
his nest and presented myself as dessert, I forced my
feet to move and traipsed unhappily through the
door into Dacara's lair.

I f I'd been expecting the TV version of the
Addomson Family mansion, I was disappointed. But what I saw was almost worse.

The house was surprisingly normal, if eclectic.
In the first room, brightly hued walls were covered
with a variety of paintings, from the popular dogs
playing poker to big-eyed children sharing a tea
party to cows gazing on a vibrant green field.

The furniture was equally eclectic, including red
velvet couches with tasseled pillows juxtaposed with
white wicker chairs and a coffee table that seemed to
consist of two fruit crates side by side with a sheet of
plexiglass over them to create a makeshift table.

The floor was marble, shiny, and bright white
with gray veining. Vivid yellow rugs covered it in
strategic spots.

Two long, black scythes, which looked like something the ferryman of Hades would use to ferry the dead across the River Styx, hung crisscrossed above the fireplace.

Disturbing.

The result was a chaotic mess that hurt the eyes and jumbled the senses. A college-dorm feeling enveloped me as I stepped through the door.

Only the massive fireplace directly across from the entrance warmed the room in more than the usual sense, taking it from crazy kitsch to cozy eclectic.

Our hostess caught me taking it all in. "Fun, huh?"

I nodded before I gave myself time to consider. "Very...unique."

She seemed pleased with my response. "Yes! This way."

I shared a look with Grym as we followed the bouncing steps of the dual sorceress across the large room to a wide arched opening in the far wall. He shook his head, his dark brows lowering with concern. Nothing was adding up. Nothing we were seeing made sense. Which, given what we'd experienced on our trip up the mountain and the fact that she'd been banished to the center of the Enchanted Forest for a reason, meant one of two things. Either Dacara was an excellent actress. Or she was truly mad.

I was voting for the latter.

Either way, we needed to be on full alert. The sorceress was as dangerous as she was unpredictable. And she had no reason to treat us with any kind of fair play.

In fact, she seemed inclined to view us as playthings rather than equals.

The archway led to a long, windowless hallway lit only by the occasional sconce, which I assumed burned magical fire. After a moment, the pervasive scent of oil and the existence of acrid black smoke made me take a closer look at the sconces, and I realized the fire they burned was real.

Without conscious agreement, the four of us huddled close together as we descended the seemingly endless hallway. The descent was gradual but unmistakable. And the further along we went, the colder the air and the slimier the rock walls and floor of the passage became.

I realized with a start that we were heading into the mountain itself. With that realization, a thick and clogging sense of claustrophobia tightened my chest, making it hard to breathe.

It was no wonder Grym, Archie, Alice, and I were all smashed together. There was definitely comfort in numbers.

I thought of Sebille and blinked, wondering where she'd gone. Hopefully, she could find her way to us before the turtle poop hit the primordial fan.

Finally, a door came into view ahead of us in the

tunnel. My eyes were stinging from the acrid smoke and my stomach was upset, more from nerves than anything else.

Grym's face was tense by the time Dacara reached for the door and placed her palm flat on its metal surface. A slim line of flame danced along the edges and the door snicked open, moving silently into the room beyond.

"We're here!" she announced unnecessarily. "Come on in."

Without another word, the sorceress bounced into the room, leaving us to decide whether we wanted to enter or not.

We shared a last, uncertain glance between us, and then Archie took a deep breath and stepped through the door.

Frowning, her chin wobbling with nerves, Alice stepped through after him. Grym glanced one last time back the way we'd come. The passage dissipated into shadow in the distance, and something shimmered around the edges. As if the entire thing were simply an illusion that could pop away at our hostess's whim.

I filled my lungs with air and touched Grym's shoulder. "Ready?"

He hesitated another beat and then nodded.

Fingers entwined, we stepped through the door together, and I immediately wished we hadn't.

24

LEAPING LIZARD BISCUITS!

The first thing we saw was a flaming prison, a pale figure lying on a bed at its center. The blaze rose straight up from the floor, flickering in fingers of orange, red, and blue fire that crawled up invisible tracks from floor to ceiling in regular, though intermittent threads. It crackled like real fire, and gave off heat, though not nearly as much heat as a fire that size should create.

The figure on the bed was male, with curly blond hair that lay in glossy strands around his handsome face. He might have been around thirty, but the pale leanness of his tall form made him appear younger. Maybe closer to my own early twenties.

The man in the fiery prison wore a strange outfit of tights with a black leather tunic of some sort that fell to just below his hips. A wide metal belt cinched the tunic at the waist and set off the broadness of his shoulders.

His eyes were closed and he appeared to be sleeping.

"Who is that?" I asked, the words wrung from my tight throat.

"Eddie," Archie said. His own voice sounded strained. When I glanced Archie's way, I couldn't miss the shimmer of tears in his dark blue gaze.

Eddie meant something to Archie. I had to find out what. His obvious attachment would explain why he'd been so insistent that we rescue Narina. Despite the fact that she'd seemed to be functioning under her own steam when she'd stolen Tildy.

The floor of the large room was formed of the same stone blocks we'd seen in the massive entry of the castle. It was clean and polished, the stone gleaming in the sunlight streaming through massive windows in the opposite wall.

I frowned. It had been overcast and dark when we'd entered the castle. And, unless I was losing my mind, we'd climbed deep inside the mountain to get to that room. There was no way real sunlight could exist there.

"Isn't he beautiful?" Dacara asked, her nearly black eyes dewy with emotion as she stared at the man in the fiery prison.

"Why is he imprisoned?" Archie growled out, his distinguished face taut with rage.

Dacara smiled, his anger sliding right off her. "Dear Eddie is not feeling well. He's in enforced rest. It's for his own good."

Archie's lips compressed to a thin line. "Not feeling well? Do you mean because he wants nothing to do with you? Or because he's done everything he can to escape your evil grip?"

Dacara sighed, looking disappointed by Archie's outburst. "It's so sad, you know. Some people just can't accept losing the respect of a loved one." She shook her dark head and her unfathomable dark eyes tightened, something swirling angrily in their depths.

Caught staring into her gaze, I felt the effects of her power as my thoughts scattered and grew muzzy. Distant warning bells chimed in my brain. I knew I should look away but found it impossible to do.

Fear clamped icy fingers around my heart, speeding its normal rate until I was breathless with panic.

The grip on my hand tightened. The distraction yanked me free of the abyss I'd been sinking into. I blinked, turning to Grym. His gaze met mine and he gave me a tight nod.

Message received. Don't look into the sorceress's eyes. Got it.

"Is he..." Archie swallowed hard, blood rushing from his lean face to leave it chalk-white. "Have you killed him?"

Dacara's laughter trilled through the room, terrifying due to its slightly hysterical tone. "Why would I kill the man I love, sorcerer?" She sauntered toward the prison, reaching a hand through the flames and caressing poor Eddie's pale arm. "I'm giving him time to adjust to our lives here. That's all."

Archie's fists were clenched, the skin around his mouth white.

"Where's Tildy?" Alice asked. Her voice was strident. She was clearly unnerved.

"She's having a walkabout," Dacara said, laughing again. "I don't believe the sorceress was taking me seriously. It seemed a good idea to convince her otherwise."

Grym stepped forward. "Dacara Wilcox, you're under arrest. Please step away from the prisoner and clasp your hands behind your back."

Dacara ignored him, continuing to stare at Eddie.

Grym moved forward, his strides determined.

Dacara threw out a hand without even glancing his way. Grym flew backward, bathed in a flash of silver light before he crashed into the wall beside the door. He hit with the force of rock against rock, and I realized he'd transformed into his gargoyle form.

Grym shoved to his feet and pounded forward again. Dacara turned away from the prison. The whirling blackness of her gaze was an angry vortex as her pixie face tightened with rage. Grym was nearly on her when she lifted her hands again and sent magical fire blasting his way.

He put his head down and took the blast, the flame doing nothing to his rocky exterior.

The sorceress didn't waste time flinging another blast of magic at the cop. Her second attempt wasn't fire.

The inky magic oozed out and flared over Grym, painting his huge form in black slime that glistened in what had to be manufactured sunlight from the windows behind her.

He jolted to a stop, his big body wavering as it fought the grip of whatever she'd thrown his way.

"Grym!" I screamed as he hit his knees and his head bowed, his mighty hands fisting with some kind of internal battle.

I started forward and Dacara's head whipped in my direction. As soon as her eyes met mine, energy leached from my muscles and my will slid away. I jerked my gaze from hers as she lifted her hands again, a mean smile curving across her pixie face.

I turned to my companions. "Archie!"

He threw a blanket of energy over Alice and me, the magic hitting me like a baseball bat to the back of my knees. I crashed downward, yelping in pain, and hit something springy and soft. My eyes shot open and I looked up at...nothing.

Archie had voided us again.

Leaping lizard biscuits!

"Grym?" I coughed out as I collapsed to my butt. "Did you grab him too?"

A light flared on a few feet away. "No, he was too close to that horrible woman," Archie's familiar voice said from behind the light. "We'll need to go back, of course. I'm just buying us some time to plan."

Good, I thought. I'd been afraid I'd have to fight them to return and rescue Grym.

Alice's softly-rounded form edged into the light. Her face was shadowed, Archie's phone light painting a sharp glare on her round glasses. She shoved them up her small nose as she peered down at me. "We need to find Tildy."

I frowned at her and slowly climbed to my feet. "Alice, I understand you want to save that tortoise, but…"

She swung a hand to silence me. "It's not that…I mean…of course I want to save her. But don't you see? She's our way out of here."

I blinked at her for a long moment. Then I realized she was right. Even if we could defeat Dacara, break Eddie out of his prison, find Narina, and escape with everybody, I wasn't looking forward to returning back outside to wade through more of those wraiths.

"What do you think she meant by walkabout?" I asked, wincing as I put weight on my legs. I peered at the other two. Why didn't they seem sore from the voiding?

"I'm afraid to ask," Alice groused.

"You heard her. She's teaching Narina a lesson," Archie said, his expression grave.

"In what way?" I asked, carefully testing my legs. The pain seemed to be softening with movement, but I was pretty sure I was going to have some dandy bruises.

"Think about it, Naida," Archie said, his tone harsh. "That turtle can cross dimensions and time-lines. If you wanted to torture somebody, what better way than to strap them to Tildy and program in some horrible spots in the universe?"

I swallowed hard as the full impact of his words hit me. "Holy Hades..."

"Precisely," Archie said. "What if that horrible woman sent her to the underworld, which is filled with wraiths and even more horrible things. What if Dacara made sure Narina was unable to protect herself?"

It was too horrible to contemplate. "But why? What's the story between her and Dacara? Who is this Eddie guy? What is he to you?" I hadn't meant to ask the questions right then. It wasn't the time or place. We needed to get back to the fight and save Grym. But the words just popped out of my mouth. And then it was too late to pull them back.

I wasn't sure if it was the darkness of the void, the shadows thrown by the phone light, or Archie's reaction to my questions, but pain seemed to glide over his features before he mastered it. "We don't have time…"

"She's family," Alice said, earning herself a glower from Archie. She shrugged. "She has a right to know, Pudsy."

He winced. "Yes. But not right now."

"And Eddie?" I asked, almost afraid to know. "What is he to you?"

He sighed. "My nephew."

My world tilted, swayed. *Nephew*? "Eddie and I are cousins? I asked him.

He seemed to wrestle with strong emotion for a moment and then straightened, shoving the pain away. "I'll tell you everything, Naida," he finally said. "But not here. Right now we need to focus on saving them." He fixed me with a questioning look. "Do you have any ideas how we can do that?"

I gulped. "Um…"

"We need to get Tildy back here." For all that she was fast becoming an annoyingly screeching boxcar on the Tildy train, Alice was right. Tildy was our best chance of escaping with all our organs and limbs intact.

I nodded. "You're right. But we don't know if she's currently in this dimension, which means there's no guarantee she'd come to us even if we called her."

"If we join forces, we might manage to pull her in," Alice suggested.

I didn't have high hopes that would work. I'd always thought I had to be within a short distance of the artifacts I summoned for my power to work. At the very least, in the same dimension. But if Archie's guess was right and Dacara had sent Narina to the Hades dimension, there was little chance we could call her back from there.

If only we had the clicker.

My eyes went wide. "The clicker!"

Archie and Alice stared at me, not understanding.

"Dacara has to have the key, right? She wouldn't have left it with Narina. It's probably in her workshop since that appears to be where she performs all her nasty activities. We just need to find it and call Tildy back."

Archie nodded thoughtfully. "Right. Okay, that makes sense."

"But Dacara's not just going to stand there and let us look," Alice said.

"No, she won't. We'll need a surprise element or two on our side."

"What are you thinking?" Archie asked.

"I'm thinking it's time we threw a sprite at a pixie." I glanced at Archie. "Can you peek out and see what's going on?" I asked the sorcerer.

He stuck his head through the blackness, disappearing from the neck up. I shuddered at the sight. I'd never get used to Archie and his void magic. He wrenched suddenly backward on a yelp, back-tracking quickly. The light of the phone he still gripped ping-ponged around the void in a manic dance. He turned to me but forgot to lift the light, so I couldn't see the expression on his face.

I didn't really need to see it. His long body had gone rigid.

"What's gone wrong now?" Alice sighed out.

"Just about everything you could think of," was the sorcerer's unhappy response.

25

SKEEEEEERCH!

"What is it?" I asked, wishing I had a window to peer through too.

"The good news is that your detective and the sprite are fighting back..." Archie said, lifting the phone so that I could once again see him.

"And the bad news?" I asked, wincing at his tone.

Archie's sigh was almost desperate. "Dacara is the least of their worries."

My heart fell. "Tell me."

"Wraiths," he said simply. "Lots of them."

Flying frog farts!

I thought for a moment. Then I glanced at Archie. "Do you have full control of the voids you create?"

"Yes."

"Can you...partition them?"

Archie seemed to be thinking about that for a moment. Finally, he nodded. "Yes. I believe I can. I've done it a few times. Though, if you're thinking what I think you're thinking, I've never tried to hold anything that was magically astute that way."

"Worst case?" I asked.

He stared off into the void for a beat and then nodded as if warming to the idea. "I'd void jump, leaving them behind."

I grinned.

He grinned back. "Brilliant plan, Naida. But you and Alice can't be here. I'll need my full focus for what you're suggesting."

Alice, whose head had been whipping back and forth between us as we talked, shoved at her over-sized glasses and pursed her lips. "I'm not going to ask. You'll explain it all later, I assume."

"Of course," Archie said, nodding.

In painful, long-form detail, I thought.

Archie held up a finger and poked his face through the void again. He jerked back a couple of times and moved to a different place each time, sticking his face through from each location. Finally, he nodded. "This will do nicely." He held out a hand and wiggled his fingers for us to approach. Wrapping long, tapered fingers over my shoulder, he peered down at me through eyes that were alarmingly similar to mine. "There's much I want to tell you, child. When this is over, I promise I will."

I held that familiar gaze for a beat, reading the intensity there, and finally nodded. "I'm going to hold you to that," I told him.

He patted my shoulder and then unceremoniously shoved me from the void.

I stumbled backward, smacking up against some kind of filing cabinet and catching hold of its slick, metal surface before I hit the ground.

A beat later, Alice stumbled out of thin air and ran into me.

"Umph!" I said as her soft body smacked into mine. The cabinet behind us tilted under the impact and then slammed loudly down against the stone floor.

We went very still, glancing around to make sure we hadn't been noticed. I was happy to see that Archie had deposited us in the back corner of the big workshop, away from the action. We stood in an area divided off from the rest by a large white rug that was anchored in the center by a white laminate desk and black office chair. The surface of the desk was a messy jumble of paper, pens, and paper clips. A few uneven piles of books were anchored by mugs holding varying levels of cold coffee or tea.

The battle was going on twenty yards away.

Dacara stood in the center of the room, her hands up and a nearly constant stream of black energy roiling from her palms. At the end of each spiral of oily magic, a wraith emerged, fully formed and seemingly pre-programmed to go after my friends.

Rage filled me at the sight. As fast as Grym and Sebille dispatched the nasty things, Dacara created more of them.

They could never reach the sorceress to stop the flow.

"I guess we know what her second magic is now," Alice said in a voice throbbing with despair. We looked at each other and I saw my own panic reflected in her gaze. Without thinking, I wrapped an arm around her shoulders and gave her a little squeeze. "We need to take her down," I said.

Alice nodded. "I'll search for the clicker?"

Without hesitation, I stepped away. "And I'll see what handy artifacts that nasty death sorceress has in this castle."

On the fringes of the battle, a slit flashed open in the air behind two of the wraiths. Archie reached through and grabbed one in each hand, ripping them backward into his void.

Four wraiths later, Archie leaped from thin air into another void, disappearing again.

I smiled. "That has to help," I murmured.

Forcing myself to turn away, I lifted my hands and called my Keeper energy forward, praying to the goddess that the Enchanted Forest's magic amplification worked inside Dacara's castle.

My energy flashed away from me so hard and fast I stumbled backward, smacking a hip painfully against the sharp-edged desk. "Ow!" I complained, rubbing my sore hip.

Behind me, the sound of drawers opening and slamming closed told me Alice was deep into her search. Papers flew through the air, sifting downward to land on the stones at my feet.

I stared toward the door of the workshop and waited, listening for the soft sound of artifacts whistling toward me—no easy task with all the chaos and noise in the workroom.

Moments passed and nothing came. Fighting disappointment, I looked around for something I could use to join the battle. I couldn't just stand there and watch Grym and Sebille get battered.

I stepped sideways and my toe connected with something metal that clanged loudly against the file cabinets from my kick.

I tensed, swinging around to discover my worst nightmare. Two wraiths had turned in my direction at the sound. The glowing eyes within the hoods of their wispy robes focused on me.

Wriggling wraith worms!

Panic twisted my guts. I tried to yank another protective bubble around myself, like I'd done on the cliff ledge outside, but nothing came. My strength wasn't in protective magic.

I'd been hoping against hope that a useful artifact would come to me. I had power over artifacts. I
was very effective with them. Thinking of Blackbeard's sword, I wished I had a blade to use against
the monsters flying toward me at a terrifying speed.

Acting in desperation, I reached for the metal
canister on the floor and braced myself, knowing it
wouldn't be enough.

The first wraith reached me, clawed hands
outstretched. The horrible slit in its center flared
wide, showing a roiling orange miasma that I knew
burned like acid. I swung the canister at its head and
managed to send it flying, though the canister flew
out of my hands along with it.

Dangit!

The second wraith hit my chest and we flew
backward, crashing onto the top of the desk and
sliding off to slam to the ground on the other side.
All the air left my lungs when I hit. My mouth
opened on a scream I had no air to voice. Horrible
wheezing sounds left my throat as I fought to pull air
through it.

The wraith's claws dug deeply into the flesh of
my shoulders. Razor-edged ribbons of agony flared
around the jagged wounds. But that wasn't the worst
of it.

Images danced through my mind, moving across
my inner vision on tiny, acid-coated claws that left

me bleeding and raw as they tore away my anchor to all that was good and pure.

Maimed and bleeding faces flashed past. Blood sprayed and dripped and puddled. Mouths gaped on unheard screams. Eyes bulged in terror.

Feelings of despair and unhinged trepidation ripped my soul wide and I screamed on the first breath I managed to drag through my fear-clogged throat. The sound was shrill and jagged and filled with every terror I'd ever known. Tears bathed my cheeks and blurred my vision.

I felt myself dying. Saw all my friends being killed. And felt the loss of everything I held dear. Despair sliced fresh tracks through my heart.

All I wanted was to die.

In the distance was chaos. I could barely hear it through the fear-drenched screaming inside my head.

In the distance, someone screamed my name.

Gone. I was gone. Everything...was gone.

A soft whirring sound filtered through the despair. The air throbbed as something flashed through it, a tiny part of my tortured mind hearing its call.

I didn't even realize when my hand shot into the air. I barely noticed the impact as the object slammed into my palm and shaped itself to my grip.

A beat later, my other hand shot up as a second

scythe slammed into it. The magic in the blades felt dark and old and extremely powerful. I didn't think I'd ever held an artifact as old as the scythes. For a brief moment, I wondered if they were Charon's actual scythes.

Heh! That was ridiculous.

The magic in the scythes had muted the wraith's horrible energy. The images in my mind had faded. And when the artifacts' magic spoke to me, I knew exactly what to do with them.

I lifted the scythes above my head and my body rose off the floor, the wraith rising up with me and floating away to stare at me through its inscrutable fiery gaze.

I figured it was sizing up the scythes, trying to figure out what they would do.

I didn't make the nasty creature wait long to find out. As the death magic saturating the blackened wood blades whispered to me, enticing me to its will, I swung the first scythe in a smooth arc that neatly severed the wraith's nasty head. Before the appendage hit the ground, the entire mess disintegrated into a pile of charcoal-colored ash.

The second wraith shot toward me. I slashed unerringly across the base of its hood, and it too disintegrated.

A presence at my back had me swinging around, slicing cleanly across first one, and then without thought, the second of the two phantoms attacking me. As if a silent command had been sent through the ranks to overwhelm me with numbers, a dozen wraiths drifted across the room on their magical air currents. I braced, the long curved blades of my scythes crossed before me.

The wraiths attacked in a blood-chilling wad. The slits in the center of their bodies flashed open and their horrible shrieking filled the room. Unlike during the battle on the mountainside, their screaming didn't affect me.

I had the scythes.

I didn't give conscious thought to moving, but suddenly I was flying forward—my steps light and quick across the stone. I swung and ducked and spun and sliced, a deadly dance that only I could perform.

I was deep in the magic zone, lost to the brutal waltz of the blades, just as I was when I held Blackbeard's sword in my hand.

It was as if I were the grim reaper himself. Or... you know...herself. Who really knew? I doubted anybody was going to look underneath those robes to find out.

Skeeeeeerch!

I slammed the brakes on that thought process before I dropped totally into the toilet of my mind.

My dance was magical and pleasing and precise. It was fast and efficient. But I didn't tire. I didn't falter. Not even when four wraiths surrounded me at once, claws slashing toward me through the air. I danced on, dusting the stone floor around me with the wraiths' ashy remains.

Until, finally, I had no more monsters to destroy. I stumbled to a stop and blinked in surprise, the residue of the magic dance still clinging to the edges of my mind.

Unfortunately, someone else was there. And I didn't like the look in her swirling eyes.

"Well, well, well," Dacara said, her lips curved into a smile that didn't match her murderous gaze. "Very clever, Keeper. I'm surprised the scythes would answer your call."

I followed her gaze downward, to the blades that drooped from my hands like dying daisies. Their magic no longer thrummed through the age-blackened shafts. I keenly felt its loss.

My anxious gaze slid past the sorceress, looking for my friends.

I sucked in a horrified gasp.

Grym was sprawled across the floor, in his human form again, and covered in wraith claw wounds. He wasn't moving and his skin had a grayish cast.

Sebille was nowhere to be seen.

I forced myself not to turn and look for Alice. If she'd managed to hide, I didn't want to give her away. "Give us back the prisoners and Tildy and we'll leave you alone," I told Dacara, my tone not as demanding as I'd hoped.

She laughed, the spikes of her midnight hair shivering as she shook her head. "I don't think so. That tortoise is going to give me back my freedom."

Understanding flared, bringing horror with it. "You're going to use Tildy to escape the forest."

Her smile was filled with childish delight. Combined with the swirling dark gaze, it made her look like one of those scary killer dolls. "Ingenious, yes?"

I shook my head. We couldn't allow her to get away with it. She was too dangerous to be let loose on the world. "You aren't getting that tortoise," I told her.

She cocked her head. "I don't think you understand your position, Naida Keeper. I'm the one with all the power here. Not you."

Unfortunately, I did understand it. All too well. But I wasn't going to let her know that. "You kidnapped Eddie to force Narina to bring the tortoise to you."

She clapped her hands, clearly thrilled to have her evil genius recognized.

"I'm guessing, since you have the tortoise now, you were planning on killing Narina and Eddie?"

Dacara frowned. "Don't be silly. I love Eddie."

"It doesn't sound like he loves you," I told her, my thoughts churning in search of a way out.

She sighed. "Goddess save us from independent men. Am I right?" Her grin widened.

I just shook my head. "You don't need to kill anybody," I told her, despair churning acid in my belly. "You have the turtle. Why don't you let us go?"

I was just stalling for time. I knew she'd never let us go. But I *had* always been a strong believer in the "fake it 'til you make it" philosophy.

When she laughed gaily at my suggestion, I tried to lift the scythes to brandish at her, but they felt as if they weighed fifty pounds each. Apparently, she was blocking my magic somehow, or maybe just its effect on her scythes. I dropped them to the floor. They were little more than anchors at that point.

My mind raced. What did I have left?

Archie! I wondered where he was. Had he ridden his voids all the way home, leaving the rest of us to figure out how to escape on our own? I didn't believe he'd do that to me. Or to the man in the fiery prison. Or Narina. I wasn't clear on the exact nature of our relationship just yet, but I had some suspicions. And if I was right, Archie would likely be willing to die to save at least some of us.

No. He had to be lying low somewhere, looking for an opportunity to do what needed to be done.

Alice? Had she hidden, or had the wraiths gotten to her?

And Sebille. I didn't see her body lying about. But then, if she was in her sprite form, she'd be tiny.

She could have fallen behind something and I'd never see her.

The most distressing thing was that Dacara didn't seem concerned about any of my friends. That didn't bode well for them...or me. "The PTB for this dimension knew we were coming here. She won't be happy if you hurt us."

She laughed again. "Hurt you? I would never do that. At least..." Her grin went lopsided and her malevolent gaze shone with evil delight. "I wouldn't *only* hurt you. I'm thinking permanent banishment to...let's see..." she held a finger against her chin, cocking her head as if engaging in deep thought. "The Jurassic era? You've been there recently, haven't you? You'd probably last a few days before you were eaten." She shrugged. "Maybe longer. You seem fairly resourceful."

Ice formed along my spine. I didn't want to live in the age of the dinosaurs. More importantly, I didn't want to die there. "The Universe will come for you," I said, my tone desperate. "I'm their chosen Keeper. You can't just send me across time without repercussions." If only my ice-covered spine didn't believe she could and would do just that.

"It's a dangerous job, being a Keeper." She made a little moue of false concern. "It's really too bad you messed with an artifact without knowing what it could do." Her faux concern slipped away in the blink of an eye. "Oh, well." Dacara lifted her hands and fire flared from her palms. It pulsed before her in a glossy, sizzling sheet. The sorceress grinned meanly when I flinched back. "Don't worry, Keeper. I'm not going to burn you up. I'm just going to make you a little prison like Eddie's. That magical tortoise should be back soon. She's probably made her way through all the circles of Hades by now and is heading back." Dacara's expression turned wistful. "Poor, Narina. The last time I sent her through the Tenth Circle she came back nearly mad from wraith poison." She giggled like a schoolgirl. "My wraiths are delightful pets, aren't they? They're very talented, as I'm sure you've seen. They can call fire and ice and they're impervious to nearly all kinds of magic." She wrinkled her adorable little nose, glancing at the scythes. "Unfortunately, you found the one magic they can't assimilate. That was very clever of you, Naida Keeper."

She swung her hands and magical fire filled the space around me from floor to ceiling. I scrambled away from the flame but was forced to scuttle back as it closed in behind me. All too quickly, she'd coated the air on three sides with fire, using the solid wall the file cabinets were on to complete the prison.

She turned away. "Ta! I'll be back after my lunch. I guess I'll be eating alone again." She sighed. "Pity. I would have enjoyed some company."

Without warning, the air opened up behind Dacara and two hands reached out, grabbing hold of her and ripping her into the void. The slit in the void snapped closed without ejecting Archie again.

I watched hopefully, praying he'd reemerge from the abyss.

But he didn't come out. Fifteen minutes later, I had to admit to myself that he wasn't coming. Pain twisted my heart.

I was living the real version of the nightmare predicted in the wraith's horrible magic. Everyone was lost. I was alone.

And I was heading back to Spiny. The thought turned my bowels to water.

The air at the center of the room thickened and a smoky stench wafted through the space. I watched as Tildy suddenly appeared, her jaws working over some kind of flower that looked like a lily and smelled like cinnamon.

My friend LA had once told me about traveling to Hades to get a flower that killed wraiths. The flower the tortoise was munching on looked and smelled like what LA had described.

I sighed. Too little, too late. We could have really used that flower a little while ago. My gaze slid to Narina and froze with dread. She was draped over Tildy's shell, boneless and still. As far as I could tell, she wasn't even breathing.

She looked dead.

My knees gave out and I fell, my back slamming into the side of the desk. Despair was a sour taste in the back of my throat. If only I could get out of that prison, maybe I could help Narina. Maybe I could help the others too.

I stared at the flickering wall of flame, then glanced at the solid wall. Like everything else in that cursed castle, the wall was carved from rock. I wouldn't be chiseling my way through that.

Still, maybe there was a hidden passageway or something.

Knowing it was a fool's errand, I forced myself to stand and go investigate. I had to do something, or I'd go crazy.

My foot clanged into the canister I'd kicked earlier. I reached for it. Maybe I could use it to bash my way through the wall. Even as I had the thought, I dismissed it. Solid rock wasn't going to give way under a small, metal canister.

Then my mind registered what I was holding, and a spark flared to life in my chest.

A spark of hope.

A fire extinguisher.

My gaze slid to the fire glimmering and flaring along the magical threads that formed it into walls. But, magical fire couldn't be doused by a fire extinguisher.

Could it?

The spark of hope flared brighter as the energy in my core blazed to life, my magic answering a complimentary magic thrumming through the object in my hands.

I had the answer to my question.

It *could* douse magical fire...*if* it was a magical fire extinguisher.

26

BOUNCING BABY BUNIONS!

A groan had my head whipping up. Across the room, Grym was stirring, his big body shuddering under what had to be terrible pain.

"Grym!"

He went very still, and for a moment I thought he'd passed out again. But he seemed to gather his strength and push away from the floor, hissing with pain. He dropped to his butt and turned to find me. "Hey," he said, his voice rough and tight.

I couldn't help it. I was so relieved that he was alive. "Hey."

He slowly looked around. "Dacara?"

Tears burned my eyes and when I tried to speak the words caught in my throat. "Arch…" I cleared my throat and tried again. "Archie pulled her into a void."

Grym expelled air, his head dropping to his chest. That was when he noted the poor condition of his clothes. They'd hung with him through two changes to his gargoyle form. If they hadn't been loose-fitting in the first place, they'd be long gone. As it was, he was barely covered by tatters. He shoved to his feet and reached for a black robe I hadn't noticed before. It was draped over a chair near the fiery prison, and I wondered if it had belonged to Eddie. It looked too big for Dacara.

I was almost afraid to ask, but I had to. "Sebille?"

He jerked, his jaw tightening. He shook his head. "I don't know. I lost track..." His gaze turned glossy, and he seemed to be revisiting some memory or thought. Judging by the way he'd gone stiff and still, I figured it wasn't a good one. "Grym?"

After a beat, he shook it off and grimaced. "Those wraiths pack quite a punch."

I nodded, trying not to think about my own experience with them. "We need to find Sebille and Alice."

Grym nodded. He narrowed his eyes on my prison. "What about that?"

"Oh." I lifted the canister in my hands. "I'm hoping this is magical. I think it showed up when I used my power. I didn't see it come, so I'm guessing it was close by."

"I'll look for Sebille."

I nodded. I checked out the extinguisher, never having used one before, and figured out how to expel the chemical by nearly spraying myself in the eye.

Bouncing baby bunions! I swiped at the white stuff coating one side of my head.

Taking a deep breath, I turned the canister around and depressed the lever. Foamy white magic shot out of the extinguisher and hit the flaming wall surrounding me. I waited. And waited.

Nothing happened, and I felt hope die.

I sprayed it some more, willing it to work. I gave up a moment later, wanting to cry. We might have gotten rid of the evil sorceress, but if I couldn't find a way out of that prison, it would do me no good at all.

Maybe Madeline could come up with something to break the prison. I sighed. Even if she could, I'd have to wait for my friends to find her and enlist her help. I'd be in that prison for hours at a minimum. Maybe even days.

At the thought, my bladder tapped urgently against my colon. *Ugh*!

I collapsed back onto the desk.

Grym came around Eddie's prison with his hands out, an unmoving sprite lying across his palms. His gaze on me was dire. "I found her." Pain throbbed in his voice. Terror made my bladder tap harder.

I choked when I tried to speak and had to

swallow hard before I could get the words out. "Is she...?"

A slit formed on the air ten feet away and a familiar leg, covered in a filthy torn robe, shot out of it. The leg was closely followed by two hands that gripped the edges of the opening hovering above the ground. A tousled head came through last, and a disheveled figure tumbled out, crashing clumsily to the floor.

"Archie!" I grinned despite my worry for Sebille. "You're alive!"

He stumbled sideways, looking as if he'd been badly overserved at the corner pub. His longish brown hair was a mess, sticking straight up from his head, and his clothes were charred and torn. When he lifted his unfocused blue gaze, I was sure that his eyes wobbled in their sockets a few times before focusing on me. "Naida."

The sorcerer worked his jaw a couple of times, testing it with one hand, and then straightened, tugging on his badly burned clothing. "Well then, let's see what we can do about those prisons, shall we?"

My smile slipped away. "I tried this extinguisher, but it didn't work." I set it down on the desk behind me since it was obviously useless.

Archie nearly went down with his first step. He stopped and looked at his feet.

"Are you okay?" Grym asked the sorcerer.

"I'm brilliant," Archie declared. "Just haven't gotten my sea legs yet." He eyed my fiery cell for a moment, narrowing his eyes. "Unless I'm mistaken..." he moved closer, pointing a badly burned digit toward the spot in front of me. "I believe that's been breached."

I glanced where he pointed and felt my eyes go wide. He was right. The wall of fire was still there, but the flames in one section had faded, looking as if someone had taken an eraser and rubbed out some of the color. I gave the spot a tentative poke with the very tip of my finger. I flinched as I did it, expecting to be burned. What I got instead was a quick, sharp jolt of pain, like static electricity.

I gritted my teeth and shoved my hand through.

"Ouch!" I jerked my hand back and took a deep breath. I'd need to do it in one quick move, like yanking off a band-aid.

"Wait!" Archie exclaimed.

I jolted to a stop. "What?"

He nodded toward Eddie in his fiery prison. "Bring the extinguisher."

I was such a derf.

That was when Archie saw Tildy and her still limp cargo. "Narina?" He blinked stupidly for a moment before wrapping his mind around what he was seeing. "Nina!" He shot forward, his feet tangling beneath him, and hit the floor, sliding several feet on his belly before stopping on a groan. He rested his face against the stone for a beat.

Grym hurried over to him. "Archie?"

I shoved through the breach I'd made in my cell, hissing at the pain. I hopped in place for a moment, "Ow, ow, ow, ow, ow!" and then shook it off. "What's wrong with you, Archie?" I asked, more to take my mind off the feeling of being slightly electrocuted than anything else.

He sighed. Grym grabbed him under the arms and yanked him off the floor, setting him on his feet. "Void inebriation. I'm afraid I hopped too many voids in too short a time."

I frowned. "Why would you do that?"

"Long story," he said. "Suffice it to say that cursed sorceress has a few tricks up her sleeve I didn't know about."

Panic flared. "Can she get out?"

"No." He shook his head, setting the crazy hair into motion. Watching Archie's curls bob and wobble made me feel seasick. "I've locked her into a one-way void."

"One way?" Grym asked, frowning.

"Yes. She was hopping voids behind me, hoping to find her way out. She could follow my magical signature, but it would take her a tick each time to find my signature and hop after me. One way voids are only passable if you shoot straight through them. If you stop or hesitate in any way..." he shrugged.

I nodded. That was good enough for me. "We need to get everybody out of here." I slid my gaze to Sebille, my chest tight. She looked so still. "Sebille needs her mother."

"Blimey!"

We all whipped around in time to find Alice stumbling to her feet from the space between Dacara's desk and the far wall. A giant goose egg protruded from the center of her forehead. Blinking owlishly at us from behind her crooked glasses, she looked like a particularly ugly unicorn.

"What happened?" I asked, hurrying over to her.

She shoved her glasses up her nose and blinked blearily at the sizzling cell I'd just escaped. "Was that there before?"

Swaying on her feet, Alice looked like she might fall over at any second. I grabbed her arms and helped her to a chair. "Sit. You have a huge knot on your head."

She reached up and touched her unicorn, hissing in pain. "Bloody he..."

I crouched beside her so she wouldn't have to look up to speak to me. "What happened? Did the wraiths get you?"

"What? No." She blew out a breath. "I was rushing to help you when they attacked and tripped over some stupid canister." Alice shook her head in disgust. "I fell and hit my head on the edge of the desk." She gingerly touched the purple mound on her head. "I'm going to have quite the bruise, yeah?"

"Yeah," I said, smiling at her. "We have every-body. Archie took care of Dacara. We need to get Sebille home. Are you okay to travel?"

She tried to stand and nearly fell over. I pushed her back and patted her shoulder. "Sit another minute. I'll come back for you when we're ready to go."

The fact that she didn't argue told me she was in a lot of pain.

Hopefully, Queen Sindra could put that to rights too. Sebille's mother was going to be busy.

"Oh, I nearly forgot," Alice said, holding up her hand to show me what she was clutching in her fist. "I found the key."

Relief touched me with soft, warm fingers. "That's wonderful."

Archie was bending over Narina when I returned. He'd untied the thick rope binding her to Tildy. Grym was spraying Eddie's cell with the magical extinguisher. "How is she?" I asked, not looking forward to his response.

Narina's eyes were closed but her body twitched violently. I remembered how it had felt to be touched by even one wraith and couldn't even imagine what Narina had endured. Archie's face was creased with worry lines that hadn't been there before we came into the forest. "I don't know. She's

in severe mental distress from the wraith poison."
He stood, staring down on the sorceress. "I just don't
know."

I watched Tildy chew the last flower petal and
had a thought. I'd explore it further once we got
home. Patting Archie on the shoulder, I simply said,
"Let's get out of here. We'll figure something out."

"Uncle Archie?"

Archie and I turned to find Eddie standing
behind us. His handsome face was pale. Lines of
strain creased the corners of his eyes and tightened
his lips. He leaned heavily on Grym.

Grym said, "He woke up as soon as I pulled him
out of that prison."

I nodded. "A real Sleeping Beauty."

Eddie's gaze slid to me. Something changed in
his face. His expression lightened. "You're..."

"My boy!" Archie wrapped his arms around
Eddie, and Grym stepped away.

"Can you help Alice over here?" I asked Grym
without looking at him. My gaze was locked on
Sebille, lying unmoving atop the small table where
Grym had placed her. She was so still. Her limbs
limp and her wings sagging off the edge of the table
like over-washed linen.

She was in bad shape. Really bad shape. And I
didn't think we had much time. I scooped her gently
into my hands. "We need to go," I said. "Sebille and
Narina need healing, fast."

Eddie gathered his mother into his arms, tears slipping down his face. "This is all my fault."

I gave Archie a pleading look.

He turned to his nephew. "We just need to get her back to Enchanted. We'll put this all to rights. You'll see."

Grym helped Alice over and settled her on Tildy's back. Eddie sat down next to her and they arranged Narina's legs over Alice's lap. I handed Sebille to Grym and he pressed a leg against Tildy's shell, nestling Sebille protectively close to his chest.

I gave the room a final look and my gaze fell on the scythes. I really didn't want to leave them behind in the certifiably evil hands of their mistress. All in all, it would be best if no one ever used those blades again.

Making a sudden decision, I sent my Keeper power into the room and called them to me. Without Dacara to interfere with my magic, they flew to me without hesitation, slapping easily into my hands like before.

I stepped close to Tildy, placing one foot on her shell beside Grym and Sebille, and nodded at Alice.

Alice started punching buttons on the clicker. We waited in silence as she bent over the thing.

A moment later, I asked, "Is there a problem?"

She spared me a quick, frustrated glance. "I can't just push the *Return* button. It will take us to Hades...or worse."

I had no idea what would be worse than Hades, then gave myself a mental throat punch for even having the thought. I'd probably just cursed us to land in the bottom of the ocean or something.

"I have to totally reprogram our destination," Alice said distractedly. "It will take me a minute."

Something pulled the air tight in the room. The feeling brought goose flesh up on my arms and had me searching the large space with worried eyes. My gaze caught Grym's, and he frowned.

He'd felt it too.

Catching movement out of the corner of my eye, I tensed. My gaze shot to the middle of the room. The air thickened, roiled, and parted in a dark slash.

A void had opened.

"Alice!" I yelled.

The ex-Keeper spared me a quick look and then jerked her gaze to where mine was locked. A mere fifteen feet away from us, the opening showed unrelenting blackness, its edges pulsing with expectation. But the void opening didn't close.

The next moment, Dacara tumbled out and rolled to her feet like a gymnast.

"Alice!"

"I'm going as fast as I can!" She jabbed buttons like a madwoman, her glasses barely clinging to the tip of her short nose.

The evil pixie's dark eyes found us. Rage turned their depths into a vortex of swirling rage. She opened her rosebud lips and shrieked, the sound all too reminiscent of the wraith's blood-chilling screams. We doubled over as the sound ripped through us, leaving irrational terror in its wake.

Then Dacara launched herself in our direction before I even had time to scream.

27

A SHOULDER TO SNOT ON

Fire shot toward us in a seething, deadly spray. On its tail were wraiths, shooting from the flames like wasps seeking vengeance for a disturbed nest. Their disgusting middles opened and the heart-stopping shrieks emerged, the sound so chilling I covered my ears and melted onto Tildy in a pile of petrified goo.

My heart pounded, my skin chilled to the temperature of ice, and tears burst from my eyes as my own mouth opened in a helpless scream.

The fire sizzled around us, its heat a living thing against my skin. Pain flared over every inch of my body, but it didn't burn. Instead, it slipped past to die against the fake windows behind the tortoise. Though their dark, horrible bodies covered the spot where we'd been, writhing and hissing like a nest of poisonous snakes, the wraiths also slid harmlessly past as we slipped into neutral space.

If my chest could have moved I'd have breathed a huge sigh of relief as we plunged into the tunnel, and headed toward the familiar sights and scents that represented home.

Tildy slammed down too soon, the amount of space we'd had to travel so short she had no time to adjust to the landing before we hit the end of the tunnel. I shot forward, crashing into the nearest bookshelves and sending the books on the top shelf toppling sideways like oversized, mismatched dominos.

Grym was an enormous projectile that hurtled into the front door, sliding to the ground with a grunt.

Alice hit next to me and the enormous wooden bookshelf wobbled under the follow-up assault.

I shoved hair out of my face and looked at Tildy, finding her munching on the wilted remains of the snack she'd left behind when Narina had turtle-jacked her.

Archie, Narina, and Eddie were gone.

Alarm had me shooting to my feet. "Where are they?" *Please goddess we didn't somehow leave them behind at Dacara's.*

Grym got carefully to his feet, still clutching Sebille. He laid her on the carpet away from the door. To my vast surprise, she eased back into her full-size form. But her eyes remained closed, and her color wasn't good.

Grym rolled his shoulders, grimacing. "They popped away when we landed."

Okay, that was a relief. I guessed. They'd made it to Croakies, so that meant they were okay...right?

My phone rang. I answered without thinking. "Yes?" My tone was abrupt, but I didn't care. I was a giant ball of stress. My stress had stress. The stress of my stress was stressed.

"Naida?"

I recognized my friend LA's voice. She sounded worried. "Hey."

"What's going on over there?"

I frowned, wondering how she'd known. Then I remembered the magical web the witches and familiars in Illusion City used to monitor all the magic users in the area. With all the weird stuff that had been happening in Enchanted, they'd been talking about expanding it to keep an eye on us too. "I take it you expanded the web?"

"Not like you're thinking. We just get a global reading on magical activity. There are no details, only bubbles of color where magic is being used. There's a giant bloom of red and green hanging over Croakies right now. It looks like Christmas morning."

"Ha!" I said, dropping into a chair. My gaze slid

to Sebille. "I'm glad you called. I was hoping you could help me with something."

Archie's head popped out of thin air and I jumped, my hand slamming against my chest. "Holy Hippopotamus! You scared the tea leaves out of me," I told him, glaring.

"I did?" LA said in my ear.

"Not you," I told her. "The void sorcerer just popped out of a void in the middle of my store."

I was relieved to see Archie helping Eddie, still carrying his mother, out of the void.

"Tell me what happened," LA said. "I'll see if I can help."

So I did. And when I was done explaining what had happened to Sebille and Narina, LA asked me a couple of questions about the wraiths.

"Those are from the Tenth Circle," she told me when I was done. "Very poisonous. If you'll remember, Deg nearly died from that poison."

Deg was a powerful witch, and LA was his human familiar.

I did remember that. "Do you have any of the potion you used to save him?" After they'd traveled to Hades to get the dulcemori flower, which means Sweet Death—to wraiths it definitely was—LA's friend and fellow witch, Mandy, figured out how to make an antivenom with the flowers. I chewed on my bottom lip as I waited for her response. If she didn't have the potion, I wasn't sure how we were going to save them.

"We do."

"Will you share? I'd be happy to buy it from you?"

"Don't be silly. I'll tell you what, Brock is coming to Enchanted. He'll be faster than me driving it down. I'll give a vial of it to him, along with instructions for how to use it. You'll need a witch to perform the magic for you."

I gave Grym a thumbs up. "Lea can do it. Thank you so much, LA. I owe you one."

"No worries. Let's get the kids together soon, though. I miss the little fuzz-butts."

Lea and her friends owned three of the five cats from Mr. Wicked's litter. Lea's Hex was the fifth. "Deal. Talk to you soon." I hung up and looked at Archie and Eddie. They waited silently, Narina still drooping limply from Eddie's arms. Sweat coated Eddie's handsome face, and he was as pale as our patients. I was guessing he had one heck of a hangover from Dacara's magic. His gaze never left me, and his expression was speculative. "I have a wraith anti-venom potion coming. Let's make Narina and Sebille comfortable while we wait for it."

The sky above me was cloudless, the moon a silvered sphere. I leaned against the back wall of Croakies, staring out at the empty lot behind the store, watching the sky for Brock. It would be hard to miss him since he would probably be a ten-foot-tall demon with thirty-foot-wide, sawtooth-edged wings. LA hadn't told me he'd be coming in his demon form, but that was the only way he'd get to Enchanted faster than driving.

I glanced at my phone. It had been twenty-five minutes since I'd spoken to LA. I figured she would have had to go to Familiar, Inc., her family's company, to get the potion, and then Brock would fly it over from there.

He should arrive within the next ten minutes or so.

At least I hoped he would. I'd used the excuse of watching for him to step away from Sebille's too pale face and unmoving body. Even her breathing was frighteningly shallow and fast. She was really sick.

It terrified me.

That, along with the constant motion of Queen Sindra and the healing fae she'd brought with her, was turning the ball of stress lodged in my belly boulder-sized.

I'd left Lea setting up her work area and escaped outside.

"Hey."

I turned at the sound of Grym's soft greeting, giving him a tired smile. "Hey."

He stood next to me for a moment, one big, warm hand resting on my shoulder. "She'll be fine," he said after a moment.

I nodded, tears sliding down my cheeks. I sniffled, scrubbing them angrily away. "Don't you dare tell her I cried."

Grym laughed softly. "Promise."

I touched his hand. "Queen Sindra healed your wounds?"

He nodded. "I'm feeling great."

"Good." I returned my gaze to the moon, feeling its magic tugging at my core.

We stood that way for a couple of minutes, lost in our thoughts.

My thoughts weren't comfortable things, and the sheer force of my worry was wearing me down. Suddenly, without warning, a sob forced its way up my throat and exploded past my lips. Once it tore loose, it released all of its embarrassingly wet and noisy siblings to the air. I shook under the onslaught of everything I'd been holding back, from the terror of our dreadful splash-down in the Jurassic era to the fears of the present moment.

Grym turned me around and pulled me into his arms, wrapping me in a cocoon of warm muscle and clean male scent. He'd apparently made a quick trip home to shower and change out of his tatters at some point since we'd returned.

He smelled wonderful, like clean male with an underlying hint of sweet spearmint. I was pretty sure that came from his herbal shampoo.

"Let it all go, Naida," he whispered into my ear as I shook and trembled against him.

I took his advice since there was no way I could stop the torrent anyway.

Gradually, I started to feel better, my sobs giving way to sniffles, with the occasional hiccup. I leaned away and brushed my hand over his damp shirt. "I snotted up your clean shirt."

He laughed. "I have more of them."

I gave a watery laugh. "Thanks." When he cocked his head, I added, "For being a shoulder to snot on."

"My pleasure."

Something in the way he said it had me glancing up, getting caught on his dark-caramel gaze. We stood like that, staring at each other in the silent night for a long moment — until we were distracted by the heavy thrum, thrum, thrum of massive wings on the air.

I stiffened at the sound, my mind returning, briefly, to the flying dinosaurs that had tried to make carry-out dinner from our soft bodies. Then I remembered why I was outside.

Brock barely slowed as he descended. He landed

briskly, wings lifted and bracing against the air, and then walked smoothly away from where he'd touched down. I'd seen him do that before, landing as if he'd just been strolling through the park, and he got tons of style points for the graceful dismount.

"He's way too cool when he does that," Grym whispered close to my ear.

I laughed, letting myself lean back against his warmth for just a beat. He felt like safety, comfort, and excitement all rolled into one.

The demon that was Brock was glossy onyx, with a face and body that looked just like Brock did when in human form, only much larger. His feathers were a deep, unrelenting black that still, somehow, managed to shimmer silver light into the darkness.

He was devastatingly handsome. And he knew it.

Smiling down at me, he grinned. "Naida. You're looking unusually soggy."

"She's had a rough couple of days," Grym said, offering Brock his hand.

"I heard," Brock said, taking Grym's offering and then handing me a vial of thick red liquid. A rubber band held a folded piece of paper around the vial. "LA wrote out all the instructions. Lea shouldn't have any trouble, but if she does, LA wants her to call."

I clutched it close, relief filling me. "Thank you for hurrying it over."

He inclined his head, fire sparking in his gaze.

"It's no trouble at all. I was heading to the Enchanted Forest anyway."

I wasn't even tempted to ask him what he was going to do there. I figured it was none of my business, though it was on the tip of my tongue to warn him to be careful. He was a big...really big...demon and he could take care of himself. Maybe just one small caution, though. "If you see any large black castles, fly the other way."

He laughed, nodding his thanks, and turned away, his huge wings lifting to grab the air.

I didn't wait to watch him take off. I spun on my heel and headed inside. Lea was waiting for me, and I had friends who needed the potion I clutched in my sweaty grip.

28

THUS THE CHUNDERING

Mr. Wicked batted at a fly buzzing around the large window. Beside him, Fenwald watched the activity as if chasing a bug was too foreign a concept for him to contemplate. What kind of cat didn't chase bugs?

I shook my head.

The fly took a wrong turn, diving close to the sill by mistake, and a long, sticky tongue snapped out and drew it in.

Slimy 1, Wicked 0.

Ugh! I'd never get used to the bug-eating thing. "Was that good?" I asked the fat green squish.

Not as good as a calcium covered cricket, he responded. *But it will do in a pinch.*

I gagged a little at the thought.

Sunlight flared brightly through the glass, painting the rug in wide stripes and touching the table where I sat. My order book lay spread out in front of me, but I was too tired to do the work. I'd spent the better part of the last hour staring at the cats, enjoying the way Fenny mimicked everything Mr. Wicked did.

It was like watching a toddler mimic his older sibling. Except that Fenny was much older than Wicked. He must not have spent much time around other cats.

That was kind of sad.

But Wicked seemed to enjoy the company. I made a mental note to have Lea bring Hex over later. Fenny would probably enjoy going on a dust bunny hunting adventure with the fun-loving pair.

I jumped when the door between the library and the store slammed open. A white blur painted the air. Hobs spun to a stop in front of me, his customary white tunic and pants still swaying with the abrupt halt. He grinned. "Morning, Miss."

I frowned at the frog clock on the wall. "Are you just getting up? It's almost nine-thirty."

"No, Miss. I've been fetchin'."

"Fetchin'?"

He nodded. "For Miss Sebille. She's had me fetchin' this and fetchin' that."

"Ah." I grinned. "How is she this morning? Is she cranky?"

Hobs blue eyes widened. He reached up and thoughtfully scratched the thatch of light brown hair between his oversized ears. "Not at first, Miss. She was good until the teacup incident."

"Teacup incident, huh?" My smile widened. I could imagine what had happened.

"She got a lot crankier when I ate her breakfast instead of fetchin' it."

I laughed aloud. I'd have to take her something to eat.

He fidgeted for a minute, his pointed ears drooping. "I prolly shouldn't have jumped on the end of her bed, though." He cocked his head thoughtfully. "Is it true Miss Sebille can thrash me into next week? 'Cause I'd hate to miss this week. I've got brownies to eat and 'splorin' to do in the library."

I shook my head. "No. But just in case, why don't you give her some space for a while. Until she happies up."

He nodded.

A loud groan emerged from the door Hobs had left open. I glanced up and found Sebille leaning against the frame, her usually iridescent green gaze slightly muted but no less hostile.

Embracing my advice with his usual fervor, Hobs took one look at the sprite and shot through the door, sending Sebille's waist-length red locks waving on his backdraft.

Mr. Wicked and Fenwald jumped down from the sill and trotted after him.

Hey! Slimy objected. *What about me*?

I walked over and scooped him up, carrying him to the door and settling him on the library floor. When I straightened, I was looking into Sebille's paler than usual face. The chaos of golden freckles stood out more than usual against the pallor. Her hair stuck up on one side in a giantnormous tangle and was totally flat on the other side, making her head look lopsided on her neck. "How are you feeling?"

She tugged on the ridiculous striped onesie she'd slept in and sighed. "Okay." She frowned, rubbing a tea-colored stain on one thigh. "Just for the record, the hobgoblin stinks as a nursemaid."

"No surprise there. Sit. I'll make you some tea."

The fact that she did what I suggested without argument told me more than anything that she wasn't feeling all that great.

I tried not to worry, though. Both Lea and LA had said she'd be as good as new in a few days. I trusted their judgment. According to LA, when I'd called to thank her for the potion, wraith poisoning was nothing to sneeze at.

While I waited for the water to heat, I opened the hidden door I'd had the carpenter add to the back of the tea cabinet when I'd recently had Croakies updated and repaired after an unfortunate monster incident.

We had to hide the good sweets from Hobs, or

he'd eat everything we had. I placed two donuts on a plate and carried it over to Sebille.

"Thanks," she told me, plucking at a chocolate frosted cake donut as I returned for our tea.

She'd eaten half of the first donut by the time I returned with our cups, and her color was better. "How's Narina?" she asked.

I sipped my tea and grimaced. I really did make horrible tea. It tasted like burnt grass and rocks. "You might want to make the next cup," I told her. "Archie called me a little while ago. She's apparently up and about, weak but otherwise okay." I shook my head. "It's a miracle. She was really scratched up."

Sebille nodded. To my shock, she didn't even wince or gag when she drank her tea. "She's a strong woman. A powerful sorceress. Now I understand."

I picked at the second donut. "Understand?"

Her gaze lifted to mine. "Yes."

I didn't get a chance to ask for clarification. The front door opened and Lea came inside, Hex bouncing along in front of her. The little gray cat was the spitting image of Wicked, except she was daintier than he was, and her eyes were more gold than orange. "Hey!" Lea exclaimed, apparently surprised to see Sebille. "You're looking better."

Sebille nodded. "Thanks for helping with the potion."

Purring loudly, Hex rubbed once along my calves

and then shot away, disappearing into the library in search of her brother.

Lea held a small bag up for us to see. "I brought a healing tea mixture for you and Narina." She looked around. "Is she here?"

"Narina and Eddie went home with Archie. I think they're coming by later."

She nodded. "I'll just make this up for Sebille then." She eyed the donut crumbs on the plate and produced a second bag. It had a large grease spot, and the rich scent of chocolate wafted from it. "I brought frosted brownies," she whispered. "Interested?"

Sebille and I gave her a thumbs up.

Lea set the bag on the table.

I got up and hurried to the dividing door. If we were lucky, we might even get to eat them before Hobs found out they were there. Frosted brownies were the little hobgoblin's favorite thing in all the world. He wasn't above stealing them right out from under our noses if he discovered them.

"I just don't understand why that horrible woman is allowed to live free in the forest," Lea was saying as I returned to my seat.

Sebille shrugged. She definitely looked better. Well, except for the tea-stained, toddler-like striped onesie. And the "I passed through a hurricane on my way here" hair. "It's like solitary confinement. She can't leave the castle, and nobody ever comes to visit."

"I wonder why," I said, wrinkling my nose in disgust. "She gave us such a warm welcome."

Sebille snorted.

"Still," Lea said, setting Sebille's tea in front of her, "she needs to be reported to the Société of Dire Magic."

I nodded. "Archie will do that. But I plan to contact Madeline and see if I can get her to consult with the Universe about Dacara too." I agreed it wasn't safe to leave the dual sorceress relatively free. I suspected they were challenged finding a way to keep her imprisoned. Given the fact that she'd managed to escape Archie's one-way void, I understood the challenge.

A fresh cup of tea in front of her, Sebille nibbled her brownie. She suddenly sat up straight, looking around. "Where's the turtle?"

I grinned. "Alice took her to a tortoise safehouse. She said she'd be gone for a few weeks." I didn't even try to hide my pleasure at that.

"But, I saw Fenwald," Sebille argued.

"Alice asked me to keep him for her. She says he's not traveling as well as he used to. Thus the chundering."

Sebille snorted out a laugh. "Turtle travel is no joke."

Lea set a fresh cup of tea in front of me and sat

down with us. "You look much better," she told Sebille. "Except for the...ah..." she waved her hand around her own light brown hair and grinned.

Sebille rolled her eyes. "I'll be sure and see my stylist this morning."

I relaxed. She was going to be fine.

The front door opened again and Grym stepped inside. He had a giant bakery box in his hands. His gaze found Sebille and he nodded, his face relaxing. "I see the potion worked."

Sebille rolled her eyes. She hated being the center of attention.

"If only it could do something for her outfit," I said, earning myself a glare.

Lea and I slapped palms above the table.

Grym eyed our tea. "I'd love some?" He lifted hopeful dark brows.

I started to rise and he quickly said, "If anyone other than Naida can make it."

"Hey!" I objected.

Everybody laughed. Sebille pushed to her feet. "I'll do it. I'm tired of sitting around anyway."

We all watched her move stiffly but steadily into the tea area and then shared a relieved smile. Grym set the box of pastries on the table. "I come bearing gifts."

I was either going to have to take up jogging, or I was going to weigh a thousand pounds.

The door opened again. I glanced hopefully in

that direction, feeling my face fall as only Archie walked through.

His gaze locked on mine. "Good morning."

Grym and Lea greeted him. I simply stared. From the tea area, Sebille called out, "Tea?"

Archie held my gaze. "Please. Thank you, Sebille, dear."

Somehow I got through the next hour. The small talk. The friendly ribbing. The massive calorie intake. And when Sebille went back to bed and Lea and Grym left, I turned to Archie with a frown on my face and tears blurring my gaze. "They left?"

I hadn't realized until the moment I saw him enter Croakies alone that I'd been anxious to speak to my new...cousin? And the woman who may or may not be my aunt. I'd gone years without any family. And before that, two decades without family who embraced magic and wasn't ashamed of mine.

Family was a precious idea in my mind. And, for a brief time, I'd thought I'd finally found some.

"She wanted to come," Archie said, his tone apologetic. "They both did."

"But?" I asked, my tone just a little hostile.

He sighed. "But, they couldn't."

"Couldn't?" I spit out. "Or wouldn't?"

He sat, looking ten years older than before our adventures. "I've worried about Narina for almost twenty years now. Eddie for nearly as long. But I told myself that their disappearance was a good thing. It meant that they were safe." He shook his head. "But when she took you away from me too..."

To my shock, there were tears shimmering in his gaze.

I softened and sat down next to him. "What do you mean?"

He feathered a gentle smile over me, blinking away tears. "You were such an adorable child. So fat and happy, so curious about everything. Do you know that even before you could walk, magical objects were drawn to you? When you were barely two months old, your mother walked into your room and found an entire magical tea set circling above your crib. Your fat little arms were lifted toward the objects, pudgy fingers grasping the air wanting to touch." He laughed softly. "Your magic was so strong." But then he frowned. "If he'd found you... any of you...he'd have used it for evil. Your mother couldn't allow that, Naida. It nearly broke her heart, but she had to take steps to protect you. To protect all of you from him."

"Him who?" I asked, feeling anger rise again. My mother had abandoned me. Why couldn't she have protected me herself?

Archie shook his head. "It's not my story to tell, child. My story is the only thing I can give you. I was to stay away from you, watching you from afar to make sure you were safe. I was only to intervene if you needed me."

I sat mutely, staring at the crumb-covered table and trying to wrap my mind around what he was telling me. "But she left me with a woman who hated magic. She left me untrained and feeling unloved and inadequate. She robbed me of everyone who might have loved me."

He reached out and clutched my hand. "No. I was there. I watched you and even spoke to you several times. I brought you a gift and a cupcake for every one of your birthdays."

I shook my head. "No, you didn't."

His smile was sad. "I did."

Then I thought of the man whose face I could never remember. The man who'd suddenly shown up at Grandma Neely's ramshackle house after she died. The man I kept forgetting. "You spelled yourself, so I wouldn't remember you."

He nodded. "You had moments of love and family. You just didn't remember them for long." He shrugged. "It wasn't enough. But it was all I could give you."

I thought about his words for a moment. "And Grandma Neely?"

He grimaced. "A horrible woman. But she wasn't meant to be charming. She was there for your protection."

His words seemed wrong somehow. And then I understood. "She wasn't really my grandmother?"

"No. She was your mother's old nanny. She was

loyal to a fault, though not the warmest soul in the world. Trolls rarely are."

"She was a troll!" My voice had a shrieking tenor to it that I regretted. Still, the sentiment was appropriate.

His smile was pained. "Unfortunately, yes."

"Why?" It was woefully inadequate as a question. It didn't begin to cover all the things I wanted to ask. But I was so gobsmacked by what I was hearing that it was all I could come up with.

He expelled air, staring at his folded hands for a beat. Then he shook his head. "It's too complex." He lifted his gaze to mine. "And, as I said, it's not my story to tell."

"That's not fair!"

He withstood my glower, ignoring the way I struggled to breathe as anger overwhelmed me. I deserved to know why my family had deserted me.

I'd. Earned. It.

He reached into his pocket and pulled out a letter, handing it to me. "Narina wanted to say goodbye."

Amazingly, he stood. "Read the letter in the packet I left you weeks ago, Naida. Let your mother tell *her* story. I've told you mine. And I can promise that I'll be around from now on. I won't desert you again. You have my word." He started to leave and stopped, turning back and placing a gentle kiss on my forehead. "You remind me so much of your father. He would have been so proud."

I sat stunned as he left, softly closing the door behind him.

Archie had promised to tell me everything. And he'd told me nothing. I was just as much in the dark as I'd been before.

"Troll boogers!" I slammed my fist onto the table, the letter flying out of my hand and sliding across the table to sift toward the floor.

I stood up and began to pace. I was so angry I was shaking. It wasn't until I ran into something hard in the air that I realized I'd sent my magic out. I turned in surprise to find dozens of hardcover magical tomes hanging in the air around me. Rubbing my head, I started to laugh.

I laughed so hard, my knees weakened and I sat on the ground. My laughter grew a slightly hysterical edge and I worked on squelching it, wiping tears from my eyes. I lay back, staring up at the hovering books. My hand bumped up against the letter Archie had given me. I pulled it over and sat up, ripping it open to fish out a brief note, which was written in a sprawling cursive.

.   .   .

Dearest Naida,
    I cannot tell you how wonderful it was to see you. We owe you our lives, Eddie and I. One day we will properly thank you for what you've done. In the meantime, will you do me one more favor? Please keep Archie close? He's a good man who only wishes the best for you. There are many things in this world which you don't understand. I know that it has been difficult for you in the past. For that, I am very sorry. But you have come into your magic as we had assumed you would. You are an impressive young woman. Please know that, whatever you think of me for sneaking away like a thief in the night, it is for the best. It is for everyone's protection.

You are never alone. And you are loved.

Yours always,

Narina

I stared at the note for long seconds, something about it tickling my brain. What was it that bothered me about her words? What...?

Then it hit me. "Goddess in a belly jiggler!"

I jumped to my feet and hurried through the dividing door, the note clutched in my sweaty hand. Behind me, books crashed to the floor as I gathered my magic around me.

I ran to Shakespeare's desk, grabbing the stack of

books on the back corner and yanking them toward the front.

The large, much-abused yellow envelope I'd hidden beneath the books waited for me on the corner of the desk. I grabbed it, dropping into the chair in front of the desk.

The velvet seat moved beneath me, and my eyes went wide. But, I didn't react quickly enough. The booger blasting chair rolled a caress along my left buttock and then pinched it. Hard.

I jumped up with a squeal and growled at Casanova's chair, sending it on its way with a shove of my foot.

The stupid chair danced happily along the concrete floor, disappearing into the stacks, just in case I was tempted to set it afire.

I was oh so tempted.

I took the envelope back into the store and sat down at my little table, tugging the letter into the light. I held the note from Narina next to the letter from the envelope.

The handwriting matched!

A memory surfaced, speeding my pulse—the conversation filling in another piece of the puzzle.

"My mother wrote the letter, didn't she?"

Archie shifted again, but didn't respond.

"Is she alive?"

"Yes." The single word was spoken so softly I almost didn't hear it.

"*Where is she?*"

He shook his head. "I wish I knew. I haven't seen her since she gave me that letter and asked me to deliver it to you when you'd found your legacy."

My world shifted beneath me, leaving me flapping helplessly within a whirlwind of memories, fears, and dreams.

My mother was alive.

I had met her.

And I had a...I swallowed as the full weight of it all hit me.

I had a brother!

The End

READ MORE ENCHANTING INQUIRIES

If you enjoyed **Turtle Croakies**, you might want to check out the rest of the series. Please enjoy Chapter One of **Love Croakies**, Book II of *Enchanting Inquiries* as my gift to you!

The heart holds the potential for great love...and a deadly need to protect it.

Love potion? Really?

I don't have enough trouble dealing with a cranky assistant, a mouthy frog, an opinionated cat, and a hobgoblin who thinks getting smacked upside the head is the best kind of fun?

Now I'm dealing with a love potion that turns a delightful human emotion into a death sentence?

Banshee bunions!

As if I didn't already have enough trouble with *my* love life.

Now I have to save someone else from dying of love.

This magical librarian gig is going to be the death of me.

Or...you know...of someone else.

LOVE CROAKIES

Never let it be said that I have a thing against heart-shaped stuff. Goddess knew I was currently surrounded by it.

Heart-shaped cutouts hung from nearly every surface above navel height throughout Croakies bookstore. Heart-shaped doilies dotted every flat surface.

Heart-shaped candies enclosed in heart-shaped tins and wrapped in heart-colored foil filled a heart-shaped wicker basket on the sales counter.

Heart-shaped cookies, sans frosting since I'd sworn off frosted cookies after our ill-fated Christmas fiasco in Croakies, were displayed on a heart-shaped platter with a pink paper heart taped to it proclaiming, "Snarf to your heart's desire!".

And, right at that moment, a heart-shaped face,

peering at me with heart-felt emotion from eyes that reflected a heartbreaking level of devastation by my lack of hearty despair for her heartfelt disappointment.

"But you advertised that 'Hearts of Bomb' would be available today." The head, covered in a stick-straight mop of Valentine-colored hair, swung back and forth under a hearty wave of literary heartburn. "You promised."

I opened my mouth to tell Holly Heartsick that the shipment of books had been delayed, risking another accusation of bookseller heartlessness. Thankfully, the heart-rending announcement was waylaid by the arrival of my own personal Valerie Valentine.

Sebille's naturally heart-colored hair was plaited into two waist-length braids on either side of her face. She surged energetically into the bookstore, her sticklike arms wrapped around a plain brown box marked all over with heart-shaped stickers. "They're here!" She grinned at my excited customer, currently hopping around and clapping her hands with wholehearted heartiness.

My shoulders slumped with relief. I grabbed a frosting-free sugar cookie, pink sparkles glittering from its pale surface, and jammed it into my mouth, wishing I had tea to go with it. Sebille settled the box on the table and opened it, pulling out a glossy paperback whose cover was a study in...you guessed it...hearts in pinks and reds. The title of the food-themed murder mystery had been drawn in font that resembled the frosting I no longer allowed in Croakies. I grimaced, but figured paper depictions of the deadly stuff would be safe enough.

Sebille plucked a copy of 'Hearts of Bomb' from the box and offered it to my gleefully cackling client.

"Yay! I can't believe it's here!" she enthused as she did a little happy dance.

I rolled my eyes for two very good reasons.

Number one, though I loved books, and made half...okay a third...all right, a tenth...of my living with the sale of them, I couldn't imagine becoming so enamored of one that my world literally ended if I couldn't get my hands on it.

And two, unlike my heart-eyed customers, I knew the author of the book personally and was finding it exceedingly difficult to imagine my Uncle Archibald Pudsnecker, a.k.a. Ben E. Nigma, as they type to write a cozy murder mystery with a cutesy name meant to bring to mind a stalky vegetable. Especially since the book that was currently all the rage with my customers was only his second. Pudsy's first food cozy, "Banana Scream Pie", had taken the mystery world by storm, selling out its first modest print run and earning two additional runs by the time the new book was released. No small feat for a guy whose previous works had included the riveting treatise, "Spatial Voids Around the World" and "The Argument For Embracing The Abyss".

"Sebille and her new best friend shoved me out of the way and I all but ran away from the counter, leaving them to it.

I shoved another cookie into my mouth. I was going to gain ten pounds before the current Valentines Day book massacre ended.

"Thanks so much for coming!"

I jerked around at the pleasant, happy sound of Sebille's voice and caught her waving gaily at her heart-shape-faced bestie as she headed out of Croakies with a tin of the candies in one hand and her new book in the other.

The door opened again and three women, all old enough to know better, bounced in as the bell jangled heartily. (That one was a bonus. Teehee.)

The oldest and tallest of the threesome set her bright, expectant gaze on me. "Please tell me you have Hearts of Bomb in the store?"

I swung an arm toward the box. "Just came. Help yourselves."

My dour mood didn't seem to have any effect on their excitement. The gaggle of giggling women descended on the box like a herd...probably not the right term...of piranha and extracted whole handfuls of the books.

Finally, my shopkeeper mojo kicked in. "Only one per person," I told them. My Valentine's Day crankiness earned me a trio of scowls, but I yanked the box off the table and held it up for them to replace their extras.

I'd like to say that I was trying to make sure every single one of Uncle Pudsy's adoring fans got a copy of his latest book, but really, I just didn't want to face off with another rabid reader with the bad news that we were out of stock. Again.

Sebille gaily made the three sales, doling out candy tins with every purchase, and then sighed happily as the three women left in a dither of excitement.

She turned to me and her smile wilted like raw spinach in a frying pan. "What's wrong with you Dour Dana?"

I started arranging the books over the table in a happy display of pink and red hearts, my lips curling. "Not a thing, Valentina. What's got you so blasted happy?"

Sebille shrugged, her thin lips curving in an irrepressible smile. "Nothing. I just like Valentine's Day."

I looked agape at my usually morose and unhelpful assistant. "Why? You realize it's a totally made up holiday, right? It's a retail holiday, created just for selling stuff."

She shrugged again, her secret smile like a dagger in my blackened heart.

I slammed a paperback down on the table with excessive force.

Sebille came over, a half-eaten cookie in her hand and vanilla crumbs painting the corners of her lips. "Still no word from Grym, huh?"

I grimaced and didn't respond. My fight with the prickly detective was not a subject I wanted to discuss.

With anyone.

Sebille nodded. "Okay, don't tell me. I'll just guess."

Realizing that letting the sprite's imagination run wild over the bumps in the road of my love life was a recipe for disaster, I sighed. "He's about as malleable as a..." The thought slid away from my brain and turned to mist. I'd been having trouble holding a cogent thought all day. I blamed the copious amounts of sugar I'd eaten. Two, yes, heart-shaped jelly donuts for breakfast, a heart-shaped red velvet cupcake for lunch, two tins of heart-formed candy, and three of the sugar cookies.

I was mood eating. And, I was in dire need of some of the stalky inspiration from Pudsy's cozy.

"As a boulder?" Sebille finished for me, snickering. "Granite?" Her snickers turned to guffaws. "A mountain?" She bent double, happy tears pouring from her iridescent green gaze.

I was not amused. "Gargoyle humor. Har," I said, glaring.

The dividing door opened between the bookstore and the artifact library at the back of the building. A blur of pale pink and white shot into the store and skidded to a stop right in front of me. The air around the creature looking up at me with oversized blue eyes was striped with cartoon-like contrails from his superfast arrival for a beat before the glowy lines on the air sifted away into nothingness.

I narrowed my gaze on Hobs, my resident hobgoblin. "Are you wearing a diaper?"

He laughed happily bouncing on his oversized toes. "Miss Sebille made it for me. Isn't it great?"

My still-narrowed gaze slid to the matching, heart-shaped spots of pale red highlighting his cheeks and then to the tiny bow in his hand. "Please tell me you're not supposed to be playing Cupid?"

Hobs cocked his head, looking confused. "I'm not supposed to be playing Cupid?" His high-pitched voice was filled with question.

I sighed and threw a glower Sebille's way.

"What?" she objected. "Customers will love him."

My eyes went wide. "We can't..."

The dividing door slammed back on its hinges and Mr. Wicked sauntered through, his dark orange gaze wide as he hit my calf with a manic, "Yeow!"

"Hey, buddy," I said, bending to scoop him into my arms. I buried my face in his fur and sucked a snout full of something small and irritating.

I sneezed violently several times, nearly dropping my cat. I sniffled, glancing at my hands. They sparkled. "What is in your fur?" I asked him.

Wicked swished his tail. Hard. A tiny growl slid from his throat.

He was all sparkly. Pink sparkle! "Sebille!"

She rolled her eyes. "Uncoil your granny panties," she said. "He's fine."

I sneezed again, placing him on the floor. "You're killing me with this Valentine's stuff. What other surprises do you have for me?"

She flipped a dismissive hand. "I'll make tea. Maybe that will calm you down."

"Ribbit!"

I looked down at the fat, green squish on the floor by my feet.

He blinked up at me, his eyes blank pools of black, like miniature Pudsy voids.

Horror slid up my spine. "What...?"

Get it off me! sayeth the irate frog. *Now!*

Enormous pink lips protruded from the frog's sparkly green face. "Oh Slimy," I said in a commiserating tone. "I can't believe she did this to you." I bent down and tugged at the lips, expecting them to be made of paper, or wax. Instead, realistic-feeling flesh, plumped and puckered, met my touch, resisting my tug. I jerked my hand away, squealing. I jumped to my feet. "They're real!" I rounded on the Sprite, who quickly turned away from me when I tried to catch her eye. "I can't believe you gave him puckery lips! Have you lost your mind?"

She hid a grin behind her hand. "Don't you get the joke? Kiss the frog, get a prince? Come on," she said as steam wafted from my ears. "Customers are going to love it."

"Ribbit!" Slimy proclaimed indignantly.

I pointed a shaky finger toward the quivering frog. "Fix. Him."

Sebille gave me a long-suffering sigh and threw a pale green jet of magic toward the frog. The big, puckery lips disappeared with a pop.

Slimy gave the sprite one last indignant, "Ribbit!" and then hopped underneath the nearest bookshelf to attempt to regain his self-respect.

"You've lost your mind, sprite," I told her, madder than I'd ever been. "What's going on with you?"

Amazingly, she gave me a secret smile and headed for the door. "I'm taking my break."

I felt my eyes go wide. "What? You can't take a break. You just got here."

She shrugged and slipped through the door, leaving me with one delighted Cupid which I couldn't let anybody see, a traumatized frog, and a seriously annoyed cat.

I sagged. Could the day get any worse?

Proving that it could, the front door jangled and I steeled myself for more shrieking Ben E. Nigma fans.

Instead, I found myself looking into a handsome, craggy face, and an intense dark caramel gaze. "Oh." I said, my wit firmly intact.

"Hello, Naida," said Detective Wise Grym, a.k.a. my maybe boyfriend.

———

Check out the entire series here: https://samcheever.com/books/#enchanting

MORE BY SAM CHEEVER

Check out Sam's other bestselling series on the **BOOKS** page at https://samcheever.com/

Enchanted Inquiries Paranormal Mysteries **(More fun stories with Naida, Mr. Wicked, Sebille, and Slimy)**
Reluctant Familiar Paranormal Mysteries
Yesterday's Paranormal Mysteries
Country Cousin Mysteries
Silver Hills Cozy Mysteries
Gainfully Employed Mysteries

ABOUT THE AUTHOR

Multiple-time *USA Today* and *Wall Street Journal* Bestselling Author Sam Cheever writes mystery and suspense, creating stories that draw you in and keep you eagerly turning pages. Known for writing great characters, snappy dialogue, and unique and exhilarating stories, Sam is the award-winning author of 80+ books.

www.ingramcontent.com/pod-product-compliance
Lightning Source LLC
Chambersburg PA
CBHW070832280626
47161CB00015B/493